THE

MAILBOX

NOVELS FOR ADULT LEARNERS

THE
MAILBOX

KATE FERRIS

CENTRE FOR CURRICULUM, TRANSFER AND TECHNOLOGY

VICTORIA, BRITISH COLUMBIA

THE MAILBOX
by Kate Ferris
Copyright © 1997 by the Province of British Columbia
Ministry of Education, Skills and Training
All rights reserved.

This novel has been written especially for adults learners improving their reading skills.
The development and production was funded by the Province of British Columbia,
Ministry of Education, Skills and Training and Human Resources Development Canada,
National Literacy Secretariat.

Project coordination: Centre for Curriculum, Transfer and Technology
Design and production coordination: Bendall Books
Cover design and illustration: Bernadette Boyle

CANADIAN CATALOGUING IN PUBLICATION DATA
Ferris, Kate.
   The mailbox
   (Novels for adult learners)
   ISBN 0-7718-9488-0
   1. High interest-low vocabulary books. 2. Readers
   (Adult) I. Centre for Curriculum, Transfer and
   Technology. II. Title. III. Series.
   PS8561.E7M34 1997   428'.62   C97-960061-8
   PR9199.3F4M34 1997

NOVELS FOR ADULT LEARNERS	ORDER NO.	ISBN
The Buckle by Don Sawyer	VA0190	0-7718-9493-7
Crocodiles and Rivers by Don Sawyer	VA0191	0-7718-9492-9
Frozen Tears by Don Sawyer	VA0192	0-7718-9491-0
The Mailbox by Kate Ferris	VA0193	0-7718-9488-0
The Scowling Frog by Kate Ferris	VA0194	0-7718-9490-2
Three Wise Men by Kate Ferris	VA0195	0-7718-9489-9
Package of 6 Novels	CPUB130M	0-7719-1757-0
Activities Handbook for Instructors	VA0276	0-7718-9557-7

Distributed By:
Grass Roots Press
Toll Free: 1-888-303-3213
Fax: (780) 413-6582
Web Site: www.grassrootsbooks.net

356-2820 or 1-888-883-4766
20
ations@gems5.gov.bc.ca
cations.gov.bc.ca
rder (no personal cheques)
made payable to Minister of Finance, and ... .. .stercard, including expiry date.

Acknowledgements

This book was written in consultation with the Adult Basic
Education classes at the Selkirk College Learning Centre in
Nakusp, B.C. Meetings with the students were immensely
enjoyable and fruitful. I thank them all.

Special thanks go to Patty Bossort, who initiated this project;
also to Richard Allin, Susan Crichton; and to Craig Anderson
at Selkirk College.

I would also like to thank Audrey Thomas, Yvette Souque,
Dennis Anderson, and JoAnne Pasquale and their respective
agencies.

Rural Route

If a person's address includes the words "Rural Route," it usually means that they live in the country, along a country road. The road is often narrow, with many curves. The mail truck travels this route.

After the mail truck passes, the mailbox is sometimes stuffed full. On other days, when you go to open the mailbox, it's empty. Maybe you're early, and the mail truck hasn't come by yet. It's possible.

Or maybe there's a letter hiding at the very back of the box.

You bend down and peer into the darkness. You thrust in your hand. Your blind fingers search along the cool metal walls of the mailbox.

But there's nothing in there; nothing to change your day, change your life.

1

Silver Lake Bed & Breakfast
Rural Route #2
Greenwood, B.C.
April 4, 1988

To Jim Bass
White Wing Charters
Grand Forks, B.C.

Dear Mr. Bass,

My husband has asked me to write to you. He saw your ad in the newspaper. The ad said that you can fly people into the wilderness to hunt or fish. My husband William doesn't hunt or fish. He can't stand the sight of blood. But he would like you to fly him into the bush. He's an artist. He is working on a painting of a waterfall, and he needs to see a real waterfall.

We live on a lake, and I have paddled all around it in our canoe, and I haven't found a waterfall for him to paint. We moved here two years ago. No one else lives on the lake. We are quite alone. We run our house as a bed-and-breakfast.

I say "We," but the truth is that I run the bed-and-breakfast. My husband, William, doesn't have the time. He has to work on his painting every day. He is a very good painter. His paintings don't sell for very much, but someday they will. William is sure of it. He paints slowly. It takes him a long time to finish a single painting. And believe me, sometimes there are days when he is not in a very good mood.

Don't get me wrong. William is a very fine person, and a gentleman. He never raises his voice to me or to our son Billy. But if his painting is not going well, he gets very low, and won't talk.

Oh dear—I don't know why I'm telling you all this. I guess it's because of your ad in the newspaper. In your photo you have such a nice face, and such a friendly smile. You look like the kind of person who is easy to talk to. I guess I'm just not used to living out in the wild, with no people around.

But I was glad to leave Toronto. And I'm glad that my young son doesn't have to play on concrete anymore. Here, he has the lake, and the dock, and the woods.

I guess it gets a bit lonely for him too.

We don't drive into the village very often. I only go for groceries, or to pick up large parcels at the post office. We have a big mailbox at the end of our driveway. But the paints and canvases that William orders don't always fit inside it.

And if I don't stop writing, this letter won't fit either!

I guess I just need someone to talk to. We had very few guests this last winter. But summer is coming. And then

Silver Lake Bed & Breakfast will be full of guests needing their sheets changed and their breakfast cooked. I'll be so busy that I won't have any time to feel lonely. This is a big old house we live in. Last summer I painted it bright blue, the colour of a robin's egg. Little Billy helped me. For days we were covered with blue paint!

I hope this letter reaches you. I'm afraid that you won't be able to phone us with your reply. My husband doesn't like phones. He says that he can't paint when a phone might ring any moment. But he will be glad to hear from you by mail. He wants to know if there is a waterfall nearby that you can fly him to in your plane. He would also like to know the cost.

Yours truly,
Helen Turner

The air was fresh with the smells of spring. Helen clutched her letter in one hand as she walked down the driveway. She began walking faster. She hoped that she wasn't too late to catch the mail truck.

There were only a few patches of snow left from the long winter. The snow lay crusted in dirty patches on the bank above the driveway. But the snow was melting in the morning sun. Water trickled from under the patches. It joined the water flowing down the ditch beside the long driveway.

Helen's long black braid swung across her back as she hurried. She was a small woman, with a dancer's small hands and feet. She now ran with a dancer's grace—and arrived at the mailbox out of breath. She pulled down the little door of the mailbox, and slid the letter inside. Then she shut the flap and raised the red metal flag on the side of the mailbox. The red flag would tell the mail truck that there was a letter inside.

Helen took a deep breath of the spring air. She would wait a few minutes. The mail truck should be along soon. She looked around at the trees coming into leaf. Something bumped against her leg. It was Potto. The dog's tongue hung panting.

Potto was old. He couldn't keep up with Helen when she ran. He had followed her down the long driveway, lagging far behind. And now he would have to turn around and follow her back up to the house. But here was the mail truck. He would have a moment to rest.

Helen grabbed her letter from out of the mailbox and lowered the red flag. She waved the letter as the truck came to a stop. "Hi."

The woman at the wheel leaned from the window. "You got two catalogs today, and bills of course. Can't help that. There's always bills at the first of the month."

Smiling, Helen took the roll of mail, and handed over her letter.

The woman looked at the letter. "What's this?" She read the address, "Grand Forks?"

"Yes. There's a man over there with a floatplane. My husband wants to find a—"

"Well, honey, it's none of my business." The letter went into a canvas sack on the seat beside her. She put the truck into gear.

"Will it go out today?" asked Helen.

It was a silly question. Of course it would go out today, with the rest of the mail. But the post-lady knew that people always worry about their mail, going and coming. She could see from Helen's glowing face that the letter was important. Helen's eyes had followed the letter when she handed it over. She must expect something to happen, from the letter. People always expect something to happen, out of the blue.

But the post-lady was a kind woman, so she nodded. "Yes, yes, your letter will go out today." She let out the clutch, and drove off.

Helen did feel a warm glow at her cheeks. She felt the lift of her heart as she walked back up the driveway, Potto lagging behind. Was it only the letter to Mr. Bass that had lifted her spirits? Maybe it was just that it was spring.

In fact, Helen felt a bit silly about the letter. She had written to a complete stranger about her life here, on Silver Lake. And Mr. Bass might not even answer. Helen bent down and plucked a blade of new grass. What a beautiful colour. She nibbled on it, tasting the bitter green of springtime.

Then she looked through the bills in her hand. She thrust the two catalogs into the deep pocket of her apron. And there was a letter from some people wanting to stay at the bed-and-breakfast in May.

Helen loved getting the mail. She loved the walk down to the mailbox, and the walk back. Walking up the long drive she could see the big blue house up ahead. The house that she had painted.

Suddenly the ground shook under her feet, and Helen gasped.

The blast rattled the windows of the big house. Helen's heart raced. She couldn't get used to the explosions.

Another underground blast rattled the windows as she hurried inside. She could hear William's angry voice in the attic. He was cursing Monty Reed. He hated Monty Reed. Monty Reed was evil, a devil. He would be the death of William!

Monty Reed was a miner. He had a piece of paper that said he could blast a tunnel into the mountain. The tunnel was to run deep underground, right under their house. He was only allowed to blast during daylight hours, and never on Sundays.

Today was a Monday. Which meant that there were five more days of underground blasting to come, until the peace and quiet of Sunday. Sometimes a day or two went by with no explosions. Sometimes there would be three or four set off in a single day. Once, Helen had been sitting on the dock when a blast went off. She had been staring out over the water. With the blast, a shiver had run across the lake, as if trying to escape.

No more curses could be heard from the attic. The house was quiet once again. Helen turned on the radio. She kept it low, because the sound disturbed William when he was painting. Then she began her morning chores.

First, she washed the dishes. Then she watered the new plants along the windowsill. She had started the plants from seed. The tomatoes and peppers were now two feet tall. Their leaves pressed against the glass of the window. They leaned towards the sun. Like Helen, they wanted to be outdoors.

By the time Helen finished her chores, it was almost noon. She heated some soup, and made toast, and a cup of tea. She put the food on a tray. She carried the tray up the stairs. Her step was light, she moved quietly. At the door to the attic she set down the tray. She knocked—just once, a single rap.

"What is it?"

"It's your lunch, William."

"Thank you, Helen."

She went back down the stairs. In truth, she glided down. Her back was straight. Her feet seemed barely to touch the floor boards. Helen always moved as if she had wings on her back.

In the kitchen she took off her apron and grabbed an apple from a bowl on the table. Then she went out the door, closing it quietly behind her.

Helen was on her hands and knees in the garden. At Potto's bark, she lifted her head. Was it that time already? She had put aside the small spade, so that she could pull at a big weed.

Potto now grabbed the spade with his teeth, and ran to greet Billy. Potto always had to have a slipper or a glove or something in his mouth when he greeted someone. It was a habit of his. Maybe in his dog's mind the object in his mouth was a kind of gift, to show his welcome. Or maybe he was just afraid to be caught doing nothing. A dog should be doing *something* when you came home.

Helen yanked at the weed, pulling its root from the soil. She tossed the weed onto the pile with the others before standing up. "Hi, sweetheart. How was school?"

"I hate Bobby Reed. He took my lunchbox."

"But sweetheart, you have your lunchbox in your hand."

"He took it and he took out all my food and wouldn't give it back. He said I was weird." The boy looked up at his mother. "Am I?"

Helen kneeled down in the dirt. The tip of her nose touched the tip of her son's freckled nose. "Yes, Billy," she said, "you are weird." And she smiled.

Then she stood up, and took his hand.

"Mom, your hand is all muddy."

"Oh, so it is." Helen wiped her hand on her jeans. "Come inside with me. You must be hungry, with no lunch. What would you like to eat?"

"I want my lunch back," Billy sniffed.

So she fixed him a white bread sandwich with cream cheese. No jam, no peanut butter. Just white cream cheese. Billy watched as she cut the sandwich into four pieces. Then she poured him a glass of milk.

"I had a banana in my lunch too."

With a banana next to his plate, Billy sniffed a last sniff, and pulled a chair out to sit down.

"Wait! I've got an idea." Helen opened Billy's lunchbox. She slipped the banana inside. She wrapped the sandwich in waxed paper and put that in too. The milk she poured into a jar with a lid. "Let's go," and she took Billy's hand.

Potto was too old to go with them in the canoe. He stood at the end of the dock and watched them go. He wagged his tail a few times, in case they might be watching. Then he bent his back legs, and bent his front legs, and lay down on the warm planks of the dock. All that he had to do was wait. They would be back.

The canoe skimmed over the lake. Billy sat at the prow, dipping his paddle into the water. Helen sat at the back, she paddled at the stern. They had done this many times before. They made a good team.

"Where are we going, Mom?"

"You tell me."

"Let's go over to the creek."

Helen shifted her paddle to the left side of the canoe. They headed straight into the sun. The surface of Silver Lake did indeed shimmer like silver.

Along the shore, birds darted from branch to branch. It was a brown and soggy landscape. Dead trees leaned out over the water. A musty smell of old wet leaves was in the air. All the forest was getting ready for an explosion of green. It would be an explosion in slow motion. Plants would soon poke up through the brown floor of the forest. Leaves would sprout along branches. Ferns would shoot up and uncurl their green lace.

At the mouth of the creek a sandy beach spread out. Helen steered the canoe towards it. Billy jumped out first. He drew the prow onto the sand. The canoe rocked from side to side as Helen stepped out.

"Right here, Mom! This is the same log that we sat on last summer." Billy patted a huge grey log lying on the sand.

They sat side by side as Billy ate his lunch. Helen couldn't help but worry about him. He was only seven. This had been his first year in school.

"Mom, will you peel my banana?"

"Sweetheart, you need to start peeling your own bananas. Who's going to do it for you when you're at school?"

"The teacher does."

Tiny flies came to visit them on the log. In the warmer days to come, mosquitoes would also hang in the air. And later in the summer, dragonflies would hover over the water, and flit off at great speed. Last year, a butterfly had landed on Helen's bare knee as she sat here on the log.

Billy now pointed to the sky. His mouth was full, he could only wave his arm. Helen shaded her eyes against the sun. She could already hear the thin cries of the Canada geese. They flew in a long streamer across the sky, flying up from the south. It was spring, and the good news trailed behind them in the sound of their cries.

Helen felt tears running down her cheeks. At last she could admit how hard it had been, cooped up in the house all those snowy months. And William unhappy with his painting, and not talking, never talking to her.

The noisy creek rushed past and spilled into the lake. It was all the snow from the winter, melting. The forest behind them dripped. The tightness in Helen's chest let go. The cold lump that was her heart began to thaw.

In bed that night she turned to William. "How did your work go today?" She laid her hand on his arm. He was reading. He held his book tilted to the light.

She ran her fingers over the skin of his arm. His skin was so pale. It never saw the sun. Even during the summer months last year, William had spent most of his time in the attic.

He needed a haircut. With her fingers Helen nudged a lock of his white hair back over his ear. William's hair had turned white in his 30's, before Helen met him. He was now 50, but because of his white hair he looked older. She had married an older man. Sometimes people mistook William to be her father.

Helen stroked his arm again. "What are you reading?"

William liked to read about the lives of famous painters. He liked to read about how poor they had been, and how they felt that they had failed. Only after their deaths did the world finally see their greatness.

"William?"

For another long moment William didn't answer. Then he sighed. He laid the book down on the bedcovers. "It's no use. I'll never be able to paint water."

Helen rolled back to her own pillow. She knew what would come next.

"Do you know how hard it is to paint water? To capture it in paint as it flows over stones? Do you, Helen?"

"Yes."

"No. No, you don't. You couldn't know because you haven't tried. You haven't stood for hours and days and weeks with a paintbrush in your hand. You don't know what it's like to try so hard, and fail." William stared across the bedroom. His lips were pressed tightly together. Helen knew that in his mind he was looking at his painting—the one that was still unfinished after all these months.

He groaned.

Helen tried to shift his thoughts. "I wrote that letter you asked me to write."

"What letter?"

"You asked me to write to that man who has a floatplane."

"Oh, yes." He was still staring across the bedroom. "Thank you, dear." But he was still lost in thought.

Helen turned away, to lie with her back to him. She drew her braid over her shoulder and held on to it, for comfort. William picked up his book again. Soon his free hand reached out and came to rest upon her head. His fingers moved in slow strokes over her hair.

Once again, for another night, Helen settled for a head-rub. Instead of being held by William, and making love, she settled for the weight of his hand on her head. Another day of her life had passed. She was safe in bed with her husband. Why should she ask for more?

William's fingers moved slowly over her hair as he read his book. Helen dozed. Wisps of dream floated past. She saw things that she couldn't grasp. A face drifted by. A warm and smiling face. It was the face of the man in the photograph. What was his name? The words "Jim Bass" floated through her mind as she drifted off.

It must have been an hour or so later. The reading light was still on when Helen sat up with a gasp. Tires squealed out on the highway. Helen braced herself for the crash. But no crash came. She turned to William. The book lay fallen to his lap. His chin rested on his chest. But with another loud squeal of tires his head jerked up—"What!"

"It's just the teenagers again," said Helen.

The young people from down in the village had a game. Late at night they drove their cars in circles on the highway. Whoever left a perfect circle of black skid marks on the pavement won the game.

The screeching of tires pierced the night. William clenched his fists. "To think that I left the crime and noise of the city for the peace and quiet of the country!"

"At least no one is getting killed. They're not shooting at each other."

But a loud crash cut her short—the grinding of metal against metal.

"Oh no!" cried Helen.

William placed a bookmark between the pages of his book, and closed it. He turned off the lamp. The bedroom was dark.

"Are you just going to go to sleep?"

"What *should* I do, Helen?"

Helen lay back down. She lay in the dark with her eyes open. "Maybe someone is hurt," she murmured. But she spoke only to herself. She heard voices down on the main road. Maybe every-thing was all right. Maybe they didn't need her.

Helen lay awake for a long time. She listened to William snore.

Her dreams were troubled. She kept dreaming that she'd gone down to the highway to help. But no one was there. There was no scene of a crash, no cars. There was only someone's name, written in black skid marks on the highway. A name she kept trying read.

*A*ir Mail

Most mail travels by air. But just to be safe, glue an **Air Mail** sticker on the outside of the envelope. You can get this sticker at the post office. The **Air Mail** sticker is blue.

Blue stands for the sky. With its blue sticker, your letter takes to the air. It ignores any weather. If there are clouds in the sky, your letter pierces them and flies upward into the blue above. The paper makes a whistling sound as it ascends.

After many hours, your letter starts to curve towards the earth. It picks up speed. It is folded like a paper airplane. The pointed tip aims straight down. Your letter is heading at great speed towards the address that you wrote on its envelope.

2

Corporal Jupp stood leaning against the fender of his car. The Mountie wore the working uniform of the RCMP: a navy jacket and navy pants with a yellow stripe down each leg. The corporal was taking notes. "You have any enemies?" he asked.

William noticed that the Mountie carried no gun at his hip. In Toronto the police wore at least one gun. But they weren't in Toronto now. They were standing out at the end of their country driveway, at seven in the morning. William bent his head, and stroked his chin. He hadn't had a chance to shave yet. "Enemies?" he repeated, looking at the ground.

Helen watched her husband. She knew he was thinking of Monty Reed.

William lifted his head. "You mean, people that I hate?"

"People who might have a grudge against you, for some reason. Or maybe against your wife here." The corporal nodded towards Helen. She looked up at the two men with such an open, eager face that Corporal Jupp had to smile.

"A grudge against Helen?" asked William.

But the Mountie was already shaking his head, "No, I guess that would be impossible."

Helen was no longer listening. Her attention was now elsewhere. She was inspecting their mailbox. It lay on its side in the dirt. It was only dented. But the iron pipe that had supported the mailbox was bent in half. It had been pulled from the ground by the force of impact. There remained a scrape of dark green paint on the bent pipe. "Look here, sir," called Helen. "This may be paint from someone's car."

"Yes, ma'am. I saw that. I took a sample."

William stepped forward. "I'll tell you who did this. It was one of those kids who drive their parents' cars out here and keep us awake all night."

"What time did you say that you heard the crash?"

The Mountie waited for his answer. His pen hovered over his notepad. Helen and William looked at each other. Each was remembering their own version of the night before. William was aware that he had fallen asleep while reading. Helen was remembering her strange dreams. There had been a man in her dreams. She blushed, and lowered her eyes.

William spoke up, "It was after midnight."

"Could you give me the exact time? Do you remember glancing at a clock."

Helen turned to the Mountie. There was a glint of mischief in her eyes. "We don't have any clocks in the house."

"No clocks? Not even one? But how do you ever know—"

William cut him short. "It was 12:30, I believe." He was ready to be done with this. Let the Mounties solve the case. That was what they were paid to do.

"Or maybe a little later," added Helen, with a quick glance at William.

The corporal's pen scratched across his notepad. "I'll put down 'Between 12:00 and 1:00.'" Then he put his pen inside his jacket pocket. "Could I use your phone? My radio-phone isn't working, for some reason."

Helen started to laugh, she put her hand over her mouth. She left William to explain why the telephone was a curse to Man's peace of mind. And why he, William, would never let a phone invade his privacy.

For the rest of that week, Helen drove into town to pick up their mail at the post office. Potto rode with her. He sat on the seat beside her, shedding hairs from his winter coat. Whenever Helen spoke to him, he whacked his tail on the seat.

"What do you think, Potto? Do you think there's any mail for you today?"

Whack.

"Are you waiting for a letter from an old sweetheart?"

Whack-whack.

As Helen drove down the main street of the village, she saw the RCMP car. And there was Corporal Jupp, coming out of the post office. He was looking at some letters in his hand. Strange. Helen had never thought about a Mountie getting mail.

"Any luck?" she called. She met him at the bottom of the steps.

The Mountie smiled a shy smile. "Good morning, Mrs. Turner."

"Good morning," she nodded. "Any luck?"

"Oh! You mean, about your mailbox." He was still smiling that foolish smile that some men wear in front of a beautiful woman. With an effort, he pulled himself together and spoke in a more official voice. "I think your husband was right, Mrs. Turner. It was probably just some kid." And before the smile could creep back, he touched his cap and was gone.

When Helen slid back into her car she placed the mail on the dashboard. "Nothing for you today, Potto, old dear. It's all for William."

Whack-whack-whack.

They drove back along the narrow, curving highway. Potto sat on the seat. He stuck his nose out the window on his side. And Helen leaned out her own window as she drove. Their faces met the fresh wind.

Along the highway, the birch trees were not yet in leaf—not quite. They still held their new leaves folded. But a greenish haze hovered around the branches of each tree. Any day now the leaves would unfold, and green would return to the landscape.

As the car took the curves, Helen breathed in the spring air. Something good was coming, something good was going to happen. Helen yearned towards it with all her heart. Something had to happen, or else she might burst. "Oh Potto, I know what this is! I have spring fever!" And to herself she added aloud, "What am I going to do?"

She cooked an early supper. William ate quickly. Then he pushed back his chair, wiping his mouth with his napkin.

Helen pointed, "You still have some gravy…"

William dabbed at his chin. He stood tall and thin and slightly stooped. His white hair hung long around his ears. Helen still hadn't given him a haircut. He hadn't asked for one, and she hadn't offered lately.

"Should I change my clothes for the Council meeting?" he wondered now.

She looked at his pants. They were paint-spattered.

He saw her look. "Yes, you're right, I should change these pants. And maybe I'll put on a tie."

As he left the room, Helen picked at her food. She had hardly eaten a thing. She couldn't. She felt giddy and light-headed. What she needed was to be back out in the garden. She had spent most of the afternoon out there. Her cheeks flushed warm with sunburn. What she needed was to be kneeling in the dirt and digging with her spade. It was the only thing that seemed to calm her these days.

Meanwhile, Billy ate his white mashed potatoes, and some white meat from the chicken, and drank his milk. Helen didn't even try to put a spoonful of green peas onto his plate.

"Helen, I'm going to be late for the meeting." William stood at the doorway in a pair of clean pants. He'd put on a striped tie.

"Do you need me to drive you?" Of course she knew that he did, but she hoped that this one time he would drive himself. William said nothing. He waited in the doorway.

"All right, let me get the keys." To Billy she said, "I'll be back in a minute. There's ice cream in the freezer."

"What colour?"

She poked him in the ribs. "What colour do you think? White." And as she stood to go, she ruffled his hair and bent to kiss his neck.

She drove a little faster than she should have, but she knew every curve in the winding road. As she steered, she leaned into the curves. Sitting beside her, William was trying to read his notes. He also tried to keep one eye on the road. He didn't like to drive, and he didn't like to go fast.

Helen glanced over at him and slowed down a little. "Are you sure that Monty Reed will be at the meeting?"

William clutched at the dashboard as the car took the last curve into the village.

"Maybe Monty is sick or out of town," added Helen.

There had been no underground mining blasts for several days.

"Or maybe he's dead," muttered William.

They pulled to a stop in front of the village office. William opened his door and lifted his long legs out of the car. "Maybe he's buried down there under his own rubble."

"When shall I pick you up?"

The Council meeting was a special meeting. The Mayor was going to bring William together with Monty Reed. The two enemies were to discuss their differences.

"You can pick me up when I've convinced Monty Reed to kill himself." William stood holding the car door open. "He's trying to wear me down, Helen. With his damn blasting he's trying to force us to leave."

Helen sighed. "What time, William?" She had heard all this before.

William looked up at the sky. It was still light—a warm spring evening. "Give me an hour and a half."

The soil smelled rich and musty. Helen worked without gloves. With her bare hands she scooped out a small hollow in the dirt. Into each hollow she thrust a tiny onion bulb. Then she covered each one. Finished, she sat back on her heels, and smiled at her work. Some of the bulbs had already had green shoots showing. These shoots were now above ground, popping up green here and there down the row.

Helen had already planted three rows of peas. It wasn't a big garden. A fence kept out the deer and any rabbits. And there was a gate. Helen loved the garden gate. Whenever she passed through the gate into the garden, she stepped into a special place, a special state of mind. This little garden was all hers. It was like playing house as a child. She could do whatever she wanted in here.

She had been so busy planting that she hadn't noticed the sunset. The evening was still. There wasn't a ripple on the lake. The sunset glowed purple and rose and pale pink. Helen gazed out at the shifting colours.

Then she saw a dark speck moving across the sunset. It was a plane. Soon she could hear it—a buzzing in the sky. As the speck grew bigger the sound grew louder. The plane soon filled the evening with the high whine of its engine. Helen could now see the two pontoons under the plane's belly. She stood up. She knew who it was. And for some crazy reason her heart was pounding

She looked around the garden. Where was the gate? She felt confused. She looked down at her jeans. They had black dirt on the knees. She tried to brush off the dirt, but her hands were even dirtier. The noise grew louder as the white plane taxied across the lake towards the dock.

The floatplane cut its engine. Again there was only the quiet of the evening, and Helen could think. She used her wrist to smooth back her hair. A man was stepping out of a door on the side of the plane. He stepped onto one of the plane's pontoons. Then he looped a rope around a post on the dock.

Helen started down towards the lake. Colours still blazed in the sky, but the mountains were now deep in shadow.

The man on the dock hitched up his pants. He hadn't seen her yet. He walked with an easy stride along the dock. Stopping for a moment, he turned back towards the sunset. He stood looking at it, with his arms hanging loosely at his sides.

Of course Billy was the first to reach him. The boy came running out to the porch, with the door banging behind him. "Mom!" He ran down the porch stairs, and down across the sloping lawn. He stumbled once, falling flat on his face.

The fall had not wiped the look of joy from Billy's face. It was still there as he picked himself up, and continued his run down the slope. But when he reached the dock, he stopped short. He was only a few feet away from the stranger, and he suddenly grew shy. He hung his head.

The man squatted down in front of Billy. In a kind voice he said, "I know what you want to ask me."

Billy stared wide-eyed. His freckles stood out on his pale face.

"You want to know if that's my plane, and if you can have a ride in it. Am I right?"

Billy nodded.

"Well, the answer is 'Yes.'"

The man stood up as he saw Helen approach. He hitched up his pants again.

Helen tried not to hurry. And she tried not to stare. The man's chest was broad. The sleeves of his plaid shirt were rolled up to the elbow over tanned arms.

"I'm Jim Bass."

"Of course you are." Helen put out her hand, her small hand with its dirty fingernails. "I'm Helen."

He took her hand within his own large paw. By now Helen was looking up at his face. His eyes were blue, a very deep blue. He was smiling at her—she knew that much. But she knew little else, except that his eyes were bluer than any eyes she had ever seen. She lost track of where she was, and even who she was. Then she staggered. Someone was pushing her. It was Billy.

The boy pulled their hands apart and pushed between his mother and this man named Jim. "When?" he asked. "Now?"

The man laughed. "Not today. When I come back. That's when you'll get your ride."

And here came Potto. He carried a slipper in his mouth. It was William's slipper. He wagged his tail at the stranger.

Helen glanced up at Jim Bass. "The slipper is his way of saying hello."

"Well, hello there." He gently took the slipper from the dog's mouth. Potto was satisfied.

"Would you like a cup of tea?" asked Helen brightly. For they were already walking up the slope together. "I never drank tea before coming to B.C. It was always coffee. You asked someone in to have coffee. But here, it's tea. I guess it's the British influence. After all, this is *British* Columbia, right?" Helen listened to her own voice. *What am I saying? Why don't I just shut up?*

Jim Bass followed behind her, saying nothing. What Helen didn't know was that her dark eyes and small dancer's figure had stunned Jim Bass to silence.

It was only when they were sitting across from each other at the kitchen table that he started to talk. "Thank you," were his words, when Helen set a cup of tea in front of him. By then he had taken off his baseball cap and placed it on his knee. His hair was light brown, and wavy. And very thick. He tried to smooth it back, saying, "I need a haircut. I've been out in the bush for the last three weeks."

"Oh? Where?" asked Helen, trying to keep her voice natural.

"Over in the Kootenays. I was flying a miner in to work his claim." He took a tiny sip of his tea. When he set the cup back down on its saucer, it clattered.

The silence grew. Billy sat drinking his milk. With big eyes he stared over the rim of his glass at this hero—a real bush pilot.

Jim was looking at Helen. She met his gaze, and grew warm all over. The air in the kitchen felt electric. She felt as if she might faint any moment.

"I got your letter."

Helen's hands flew to her cheeks, "Oh god." She flushed even hotter. "That letter! You must have thought I was crazy. Only someone crazy would go on and on like I did, writing to a perfect stranger."

"Yeah. I liked it." Jim Bass reached to his shirt pocket, "I have it right here." He drew out the letter.

Helen stared at it. That was her handwriting. Seeing her letter in his large hand gave her a strange feeling. She felt close to Jim Bass. She felt as if he already knew her.

He turned the letter in his fingers. "I found it in my mailbox when I got back from the Kootenays this afternoon. So I fueled up the plane and came on over."

"But how did you find us?"

"That part was easy. You said you'd painted your house blue. And you talked about a silver lake. What was it you said—" He started to open the letter to find the passage.

"No!" Helen rose from her chair and reached across the table. "No, don't read me my own words!"

Smiling, he held the letter away from her. "This is my letter now. Letters belong to the person that they're written to."

"That's not true. Letters belong to the writer. I'm sure it's the law." She wiggled her fingers, stretching her arm even farther.

"You're not getting this," he said, smiling. He slipped the letter back into his shirt pocket. "Beside, most people around here get cabin fever in the winter. It makes them do strange things." His blue eyes twinkled. "Sometimes they even write long letters to strangers."

Helen sat back in her chair. She reached over her shoulder for her long braid. Without thinking, she began to chew on the tip of her braid. She was staring at his shirt pocket. She could see the edge of her letter sticking out. She had written it to a man she didn't know, named Jim Bass. And now that man was here, at her kitchen table. He was real. He was so very real, and breathing, and looking at her.

"I've never known anyone with such long hair," he said now.

Helen looked down at her braid. The tip of it was in her mouth. It was a childhood habit. She was a grown woman of 32. What was she doing chewing on her braid!

She tossed it back over her shoulder, blushing.

"Has your hair always been so long?"

"Longer," Helen murmured.

"How long?" he asked, in a voice as quiet as her own.

She spoke shyly. "Down to my knees."

"Oh." The crack in his voice betrayed him. Whenever a pretty woman ties her hair up or pins it back or twists it into a braid, a man can't help what comes to his mind. He sees himself letting down her hair. He sees himself untying the ribbon, or taking out the pins, or undoing the braid. He can't help it. It's just what comes to mind.

Billy had finished his glass of milk. His wide-eyed gaze now shifted from the bush pilot to his mother. She was acting so strange. But Billy couldn't keep his eyes off his hero for long. The bush pilot was talking again.

"Your husband…"

At these words, Helen felt a shock go through her body. She had forgotten all about William. Since Jim Bass had sat down at her kitchen table, she had forgotten that she even had a husband. She felt shame and guilt wash over her. "Yes… William," she choked out.

"Your husband, William…" Jim turned his head to look out the window. It was the only way that he could talk business. He couldn't look at her. He had to turn his head away, and look out into the last of the evening. Then his mind could clear, and he could think straight. "I can fly him to a place I know, a beautiful waterfall… But when? Let me think… What day is today?"

"It's Friday!" Billy piped up. "No school tomorrow."

"Billy, honey, wipe your mouth."

"Do I have a milk mustache?"

"Yes, you do."

Jim Bass turned his head from the window. He looked at the boy. He watched him run his tongue over his white upper lip. "I'm busy tomorrow. I have to work on the plane's motor. But I can come back on Sunday and fly him into the bush." Jim finally dared to glance at Helen. "Is he here? Can I talk to him?"

"Who?"

"Your husband."

"Of course. My husband William. He must be up in the attic, painting. He's often up there for hours and hours."

"No, Mom. You drove him into town."

Jim Bass pushed back his chair from the table. "Well, I guess I had better be going."

All this time, William's slipper had rested on Jim's knee. After taking it from Potto's mouth, the slipper had stayed in his hand, forgotten. And then it had balanced on his knee beside his baseball cap.

Now, as Jim slowly stood up from his chair and put his cap on his head, the slipper fell to the floor. Again without thinking, he bent to pick it up. Then he stood there, tapping the slipper against his pant leg. He allowed himself a last look at Helen. "Thank you…" He looked down at the table, and saw his teacup there. "Thank you for the tea."

Billy sat up and leaned far across the table, peering into the teacup. "You didn't drink it."

"No. No, I don't drink tea," he said, as if just now remembering that fact. He looked down at the slipper in his hand. He didn't seem to know where it had come from. He set the slipper on the windowsill.

Helen and Billy followed him out.

Potto stayed where he was, under the table. When the door opened to the evening air, he lifted his head. Then he lowered it again to his paws, and dozed. It's nice to doze when people around you are talking. It's also nice to doze when it's quiet.

The engine roared as the white floatplane turned on the water. Billy squinted at the name painted on the plane's tail. He sounded out the letters: "Dra...gon...fly." Then he yelled over the noise of the plane. "Dragonfly!"

The floatplane taxied faster and faster over the lake's surface. Then it lifted on its wings. The engine noise changed to a different pitch, then slowly faded into the darkening sky.

Helen stood on the dock. She watched the plane become only a speck again. A silent speck. "Sunday," she murmured. "He said he'd be back on Sunday." She stared into the sky for a long time.

"Helen!"

Someone was calling her.

"Do you know what the Village Council told me?"

Helen turned. It was William, shouting to her as he walked down the slope. "They told me to plant fruit trees—an orchard. I'm supposed to plant an orchard!" His long thin legs lifted at the knees as he picked his way down. "They said that if I plant an orchard all over our property, Monty Reed will have to pull back his mining operation. It's the law. No one is allowed to tunnel under an orchard."

"That's wonderful, William." Her mind reeled in confusion. She must have been dreaming this last hour. And now she was back in the real world.

"Wonderful? It's a damned insult. And it's a grave mistake. The Council tosses me a crumb and expects me to swallow it."

"But we're beyond the village limits, William. And we knew that this place had a mining claim on it. We knew that when we bought it."

"Whose side are you on, Helen?" William stopped short of the dock.

Helen could see his white hair in the twilight, though his face was in shadow. She answered quietly. "I'm on the same side that I've always been on." But there was a sting of anger in her voice.

"Come, my dear. I'm sorry." William stepped out onto the dock. He put his arm around Helen. He was so much taller than she was. His arm weighed on her shoulders.

"Who brought you home?" she found herself asking.

"The Mayor did. He's a nice young fellow. He said that—"

"Dad?"

"The grown-ups are talking, Billy." William turned back to Helen. "The Mayor said that Monty is in Vancouver."

"So he missed the meeting."

"Yes, of course Monty missed the meeting. And his absence explains why we've had no underground blasts for the last—"

"Dad? Did you see the plane?"

"Billy!"

"He's just excited, William." Helen reached out for Billy's hand as he walked beside her. The three of them were heading up to the house. The house was dark. There was no light on inside.

"Yes, Helen, I know that Billy's excited, but that's no excuse for him to talk when I'm talking."

"He's excited about Mr. Bass." Helen's heart skipped a beat, as she said the name. And she dared it again: "Mr. Bass—the bush pilot."

"Ah, of course. The good fellow who will show me my waterfall. Yes, I remember now, I heard a plane during the Council meeting. So that was his plane. Where is he, this Mr. Bass?"

"He's gone, Dad."

"Gone?"

"He's coming back on Sunday," said Helen, trying to keep an even voice.

"When Sunday? Sunday morning? Sunday afternoon?"

"He just said Sunday."

"Tell me my story now." Billy leaned back against his pillows. Helen tucked the blanket around him, and sat on the edge of his bed. "Did you brush your teeth?"

Billy grinned to show her his clean teeth.

"All right. What story would you like?"

"Tell me the story of Silver Lake."

"Once upon a time, a long time ago…" This story was one of Billy's favorites. Helen herself had made it up one night. It told of a miner working underground, like a mole in his tunnel. The miner was following a seam of silver through the rock. He chased the seam of silver with his pickax. It took him many days. Finally one day he was sure: the next swing of his pick would split the final rock. The rock would open to reveal a huge cave filled with silver…

"Silver dollars," piped Billy.

"Yes. But when the miner's pick pierced the rock, water spurted out. And to save himself from drowning, the miner had to plug the hole. He plugged it with a little rock. And then he went back home, tired and sad. And still poor."

"But what the miner didn't know…" Billy knew the story by heart.

"Yes, the water that had spurted through the hole was not ordinary water. It was liquid silver. And it came from Silver Lake. And he could have been rich."

"Like we are," said Billy.

"Yes. Like we are," said Helen, and bent to kiss him.

Billy grabbed her arm before she could rise. "One more story, *please*."

"Sweetheart, I have to go take a shower."

"Just a little one, a teeny-weeny story."

"How long? Three inches? Four inches?"

"Four."

"All right, four inches long it shall be. Do you want it to swim, or to fly?"

"Fly!"

"It's four inches long and it flies. Now, what colour should it be? No, never mind. I know the answer to that." She pulled the covers up to Billy's chin. "Once upon a time, there was a white dragonfly.

He was all alone. He was the first dragonfly of summer. He'd arrived early, and there were no other dragonflies on the lake…"

Helen now found herself speaking in a whisper. But why? Who was it that she didn't want to hear? What was wrong with telling her son a bedtime story?

"The white dragonfly darted through the air on his long wings," she continued. "He hovered over lily pads. He skimmed over the mud along the shore. As the weeks went by he began to see blue dragonflies, and green dragonflies. But he saw no dragonfly who was just like him."

Helen could feel her cheeks getting warm. Into her mind popped the image of a white plane, with the word "Dragonfly" painted on its tail. She realized who she was talking about.

She stood up. "To be continued," she said, in a normal voice.

"Wait!"

"Shhh. What is it?"

"You have to kiss me."

"But I already did."

"Yes, but then you talked. You have to kiss me the *very last thing*."

So she pressed another kiss to his freckled brow. Then she put her finger to her lips, and backed out of the room.

In the bathroom she turned on the faucet in the tub. She only turned on the hot water, so that steam would quickly blur the mirror. She didn't want to see her face in the mirror. She knew she wouldn't be able to look herself in the eye.

She stepped from her shoes, and slipped off her clothes. She twisted her long braid and pinned it on top of her head. Then she sat on the edge of the tub to turn on the cold water tap. The cooler water blended with the hot. She tested it. Warm water poured over her fingers. The water poured forth, in a never-ending stream.

Suddenly she realized she'd been daydreaming. How long had she been sitting here naked on the edge of the tub? She stood up, and turned the lever for the shower. Stepping in under the spray, she pulled the curtain around the tub. William always took quick showers. He said there was no need to waste water and time. He expected Helen and Billy to follow his example. But tonight, Helen's thoughts wandered.

The bathroom slowly filled with a white fog.

Helen continued to daydream. Standing under the spray of warm water, she allowed herself to picture a man with broad shoulders, standing on the dock.

A sharp knock rapped at the door. It was William, calling in a sharp voice. "Helen? You've been in there a long time."

$\int tamps$

In a small town or a village, you usually don't have to wait in line. You just step up to the counter of the post office to buy your stamps. You can buy a little booklet, with 10 stamps inside. Each stamp bears the likeness of Queen Elizabeth, grey-haired and with her lips pursed tight.

Carefully tear off a single stamp from the sheet of stamps inside the booklet. Then you have to wet the stamp. There's a tiny dish on the counter that holds a damp sponge. You can wipe the stamp across the sponge.

Or if the letter is going to someone that you've just fallen in love with, you might part your lips and touch the stamp to your tongue. The taste of the glue will linger for a while.

Next you press the stamp to the letter, in the upper right-hand corner of the envelope. That's where the Queen goes.

On the wall of the post office there's a picture of Elizabeth when she first became Queen. Her face is so radiant. She's only beginning her reign. With her crown and her bare young shoulders, she smiles down at her subjects. She makes it easy to believe in the romance of the monarchy.

So you surrender your letter to the mail slot, and cast a last glance upward at the Queen. She seems to be smiling on your fate.

3

Sunday morning, a teenage boy knocked on the door of the Silver Lake Bed & Breakfast. He knocked again, and then yelled out, "Mr. Turner, I can't find the shovel!"

Helen opened the door. She put her finger to her lips.

"Oh. Sorry, Mrs. Turner. Is he still asleep?"

"My husband is painting, Rex."

This was the second day that Rex had been working for them. Helen had asked the woman at the post office if she knew of a strong boy, one who needed work. The woman had suggested Rex.

Rex now stood on the porch. At 17, he was tall and wiry, with black hair curled close to his head. He usually had a ready grin, but not today. And the smell of stale beer was on his breath. "I can't find the shovel."

"Maybe you left it down by the mailbox."

"No ma'am, I looked."

Rex's job was to dig a new and deeper hole for the mailbox post. It was certainly taking him a long time. Helen pulled her robe around her. "I might have put it away myself," she said. "I haven't been thinking very clearly lately." She walked barefoot down the porch steps, and started towards the tool shed. She had to stop and wait for Rex to catch up. He was walking very slowly, dragging his feet.

She couldn't help but smile. "You act like you have a hangover, Rex."

The boy stopped, and hung his head in mock shame. Helen had to laugh.

Then she noticed the car parked in the driveway. It was a dark green Camaro. "I thought you didn't have a car, Rex." Yesterday she'd had to pick him up and take him home. The teenager's face reddened. Under her searching look he shifted from one foot to the other, acting guilty. "It's my parent's car."

At that moment the attic window flew open. William poked his head out, leaning both hands on the sill. "When will you finish digging that hole, young man?"

"Maybe today, sir."

"What?" William took out one earplug; he often wore earplugs when he was painting. "What did you say?"

"Could be today, Mr. Turner," the boy shouted up.

William nodded, "Good. And then you can mix up some concrete. Mix it in the wheelbarrow."

"Concrete, sir?"

"Yes, to secure the new post."

"But I thought I only had to dig a hole to earn the 10 dollars."

William shook his head in disgust. "Whoever rammed that

mailbox is going to be sorry," he muttered to himself. Then he called down, "Helen, you deal with him." And the attic window slammed shut.

Rex didn't carry the shovel on his shoulder. He dragged it behind him down the driveway. The shovel's blade scraped along on the dirt and gravel.

Helen watched him go. All the birch trees along the driveway were now in full leaf. She dared a quick glance at the sky—no plane—before she turned back to the house. She would put on a dress, the one printed with tiny green stripes. And she would finish braiding her hair. She'd been holding the end of the loose braid ever since the teenager's knock at the door.

But at least the kitchen was clean. Indeed, the whole house was spotless.

Upstairs in the bedroom, Helen pulled the dress on over her head. She zipped up the side. She could hear William's steps coming down from the attic. He stood in the doorway. He was wiping his hands on a rag. Helen could smell the paint thinner on the rag. It was a harsh odor. It filled the room.

William was looking at her. He frowned, saying, "That looks nice."

Helen blushed, as if she'd been caught doing something wrong. She could only stammer, "It's Sunday."

But William's frown had another cause. "I can't work, Helen. I'm just too jumpy." He paced the room. "When is that fellow with the plane coming?"

"You already asked me that an hour ago."

"Did I? And what did you say?"

"I said that I didn't know."

"Oh." William continued pacing. He shook his head, "That kid out there… What's his name?"

"Rex."

"I don't trust him. He pretends to smile at me, but it's really a smirk. He has no respect, Helen. I want you to go check on him. Make sure that the hole is straight, and it shouldn't be too wide. Did he take the wheelbarrow, like I told him to? No?"

"William, just relax."

"Don't tell me to relax, it only makes me more nervous." But he stopped his pacing. "You're right. I should relax." He drew a deep, long breath, and let it out. He forced a thin smile. "I'm going down to wait on the dock." He leaned over and gave Helen a peck on the mouth.

She didn't know it was going to be a peck. She thought it was going to be a kiss. But William's lips were gone as soon as they had touched her own. She stood looking after him. At the bedroom door, he stopped. "Be sure that you check on what's-his-name."

"Rex."

"Rex. And take the wheelbarrow." William smiled, showing the pink of his lips. "That new steel post will be buried three feet into concrete. If someone runs into it, they won't leave just a little green paint behind."

Helen held the post upright. Her legs straddled the hole. Her dress was pulled taut from one knee to the other. Rex was holding the level against the post. "Ready?" he asked.

As Helen nodded, her braid moved up and down her back. She kept her eyes on the little bubble inside the level. Rex was slowly wrapping wire around the post, to secure it.

"Oh Rex, please hurry up."

The teenager replied with mock importance. "Ma'am, you don't hurry a great artist."

And though she was straddling a hole, Helen laughed. The boy was a natural comic. Even the way he moved was funny. So slow and droopy. But his mind was quick. "What grade are you in at school, Rex?"

"No grade. I finished all my classes except one."

"But I thought you were still in high school."

"True. You can find me there."

"What did you fail—Math?"

"No, I flunked Machine Shop. The teacher didn't like my bird-house." Rex was now shoveling wet concrete into the hole.

"Please, don't splash, this is my favorite dress."

"Don't worry, ma'am. This is the first time that I've ever done this." He let the grey stuff dribble from the shovel into the bottom of the hole.

"May I let go of this post now?"

"I think not."

"Shhh! I think that's him." Helen tilted her ear to listen.

"Who would that be?"

"Never mind, Rex. Can't you just pour the whole batch of concrete in at once? Just tip up the wheelbarrow."

"Ma'am, that would splash your lovely dress."

"Damn." She tilted her head back, to look up at the sky. It was the Dragonfly—and here it came!

The white floatplane roared overhead and disappeared beyond the trees.

"Rex!" she shouted. "I'll pour the concrete. You hold this post."

Helen was small, but with strong arms. Even so, she couldn't lift the full wheelbarrow. She grabbed the shovel, and began shoveling the cement into the hole. She worked fast. As she worked she could hear the plane. It was already landing on the lake!

Rex was grinning at her as she worked. A crazy woman. But she didn't care what he thought. Shovelful after shovelful of concrete filled the hole. When she was done she threw the shovel into the empty wheelbarrow. "Wash those, Rex." She rinsed her hands in the water in the ditch. Then she set off at a run, holding her skirt up. She could hear the plane's engine grow louder. At the top of the driveway she had a view down to the lake. She paused, out of breath, her heart racing. She watched the plane lift from the water, and bank to the south in a long curve.

Down at the end of the dock sat Potto. Billy sat beside him, with his arms flung around Potto's neck as they watched the plane ascend.

Potto's tail lay limp. It wasn't that the dog was sad to be left behind. He had no wish to go up in the noisy plane. In truth, Potto was quite happy to be where he was, on the warm dock, in the sunshine. No, it was Billy who was sad. And a wagging tail would be out of place.

William sat hunched on a mossy cliff. With one hand he clutched the tiny pine tree growing out of a rock above his head. With his other hand he braced himself on his slippery perch. He should have worn shoes with a better grip to the soles. Already he worried about climbing down. But he mustn't think about that. He would climb down somehow. What mattered was the waterfall. Its mighty roar filled the canyon.

William was a man who disliked noise. He couldn't bear any sharp, sudden noise, like the shrill ring of a telephone or the blare of a car horn. Any sharp, loud sound always pierced him like a knife.

Now the steady thunder of the waterfall filled his senses. Its roar drowned "like" or "dislike." The river pouring over the cliff fell with a massive power that was hard to believe. As the water shot out and down, it sent mist into the air. William's cheeks were damp from the mist. His white hair hung wet and dripping.

He was watching the plunge of the waterfall. He tried to catch it with his eyes. He tried to hold it in his vision, so that later he could paint it. But over and over the water fell past and was lost in clouds of foam in the pool below.

William tightened his grip on the little pine tree. Then he dared to look down—far down. The roar rose into his ears. He gripped the tree even tighter. He had tied a scarf around his neck before leaving the house, to guard against getting a chill. The scarf was now soaked wet with mist but William didn't notice. He was over-come with awe and fear as he stared far down to the foam and rapids below. It almost seemed as if the water wasn't moving. Despite the flow, there was an overall pattern that didn't change. The pattern held still, and the river moved *through* it. And that's what he had to capture. That's what he had to paint.

All right. He could leave now. Slowly he stood up—but one foot slipped and he grabbed the shaking pine with both hands. There was no use to call for help. His voice would be drowned by the thunder of the waterfall. And the only person around was the fellow inside the floatplane below. What's-his-name.

It is always easier to climb up a steep path, than to climb down. William began to slide, against his will. The little pine was now stretched as far as its root would allow. William had to let go, and slide down the mossy bank. By the time he got to the bottom, his hands and the seat of his pants were black with mud.

The pilot was waiting. He'd been keeping the engine running, to hold the plane against the river's current.

William wiped his muddy hands against his shirt. He stared up for one last moment at the waterfall as it thundered down.

But he had to go. Every minute that passed was costing him money. He brushed at the mud on his pants. Then he picked his way along the riverbank. His shoes slipped on the round stones as he waded in. As he neared the plane, the pilot leaned out and stretched forth his arm to lend a hand. William ignored him. He jumped across to the plane's pontoon, and climbed in by himself. He was dirty and wet and cold.

There was a towel covering the seat. And another towel was handed to him by the pilot—Jim. Jim was the fellow's name.

"Thank you," said William. First he dried his long fingers. He tried to appear calm, but inside he felt a giddy excitement. Through the front windshield of the plane he could still see the waterfall.

"You didn't look too happy up there on the cliff, Mr. Turner."

"Pardon me?"

"I said that you looked none too happy, up on the cliff."

William yanked at his wet scarf. "It's not always easy to judge another man's happiness." He could feel the pilot looking at him.

The man continued to look at him. Then he shook his head. "No, I guess not."

When they were in the air, the pilot turned to him again. "I'm curious. Why didn't you bring along your paintbrush and canvas? There's room in the back of the plane," and he jerked his thumb over his shoulder. "You didn't even bring a camera, so that you could record what you saw."

William tapped his own forehead. "It's in here. I have the waterfall in here, in my mind's eye."

Jim Bass nodded. "I see."

"I doubt that you do. Most people don't understand what art is, or where it comes from."

Whenever William talked about painting, he became heated. His voice now rose, and he stabbed the air with a long finger. "What an artist puts on the canvas is not real life. It's more than life. He paints the power *behind* the waterfall."

Jim smiled to himself, but his voice was polite. "So a painter plays God."

William pressed his lips together in a tight line. He would say no more on the subject. He took a deep breath, to calm himself.

"Your wife told me that you're a well-known painter."

William snapped his head around. "Did she say that?"

"Well, maybe she said something like you're a really good painter."

William leaned back in his seat. "I've sold a few canvases." He folded his long fingers together on his lap. "But that's not the reason I paint."

"No?" said Jim. There was now an edge to his voice. "I just figure that most people have to work for a living."

"Mr. Bass, I worked for 30 years in the advertising business in Toronto. I know what it is to work for a living."

The plane banked in a steep curve towards the north. The earth tilted. William's stomach lurched.

The pilot brought the plane back to level. "I'm sorry if you feel that I insulted you, Mr. Turner. That was not my intention."

William stared out the side window. He didn't want to talk to this man. He didn't want to lose the waterfall. He wanted to hold on to its pattern and stillness, beneath its thunder and mist. What he wanted was to be back home in his attic, painting.

For the rest of the trip the two men did not speak. By necessity they sat next to each other in the plane's cabin. But their thoughts were miles apart as they landed at Silver Lake.

Standing on the dock, William brought out his wallet. He didn't look at Jim Bass. Instead he squinted at the sun, in order to judge the time. "I guess we were gone no more than 50 minutes."

Jim glanced at his watch. "I'd say you were right."

Jim Bass folded the bills and tucked the money into his back pocket. He hitched up his pants. He was a man who liked most people. Treat people with kindness and they'll be kind to you in return. That was his motto. But William Turner had proved an exception. How could a woman bear to be married to someone like that? Jim shook his head.

He watched William hurrying up the slope to the house. A big house. And such a pretty blue—as pretty as the woman who'd painted it. Jim felt himself being drawn towards that house. But he only went where he was invited.

Still, he didn't feel like leaving. He pulled a pack of Lifesavers from his pocket. He thrust one into his mouth, then another. He had to admit it: he'd been looking forward to today, on the chance that he would see Helen again. Mrs. Turner.

The floatplane rocked on the water. A breeze stirred the lake. The breeze caused the birch trees along the shore to flutter their new leaves.

Jim chewed on his Lifesavers. His stomach rumbled. It must be getting close to lunch time. There must be something to eat in the plane. He started towards it.

"Wait!"

Gladly. He turned. She was coming down the slope. He'd never seen anyone move with such grace. She seemed almost to float. Of course he had hoped that if he hung around long enough, she would come down to the dock. And here she came. It was strange: whenever he looked at this woman, his heart came alive.

It had been two years since his wife had died. In those two years he had stayed away from women. His pain had been too fresh. But whenever he was near Helen Turner, his heart felt whole again. She was beautiful, of course. But there was a purity about her that lifted his spirit—just to look at her. And yet she was another man's wife.

Helen arrived breathless to stand before him.

"Did your husband get what he wanted?"

"William?" she laughed. "He didn't say a word. He rushed right past me. He's already up in the attic, painting. So I think the answer is yes. Yes, he got his waterfall."

Helen turned her head to look around the shore. "Have you seen my son?"

"He was here on the dock when we took off."

"I know. He was feeling a bit sad." She looked over her shoulder again. "He was hoping for a ride."

"But it was your—" Jim stopped himself. He'd been going to say it was her husband who didn't want the boy along.

Something must have shown on his face, because Helen then reached out and touched his wrist. "I know," she said quietly. "It's not your fault."

At the touch of her fingers a thrill ran over his skin.

"Billy?" she called. To Jim she said, "I guess I shouldn't be worried." She turned again, and scanned the slope. She shaded her eyes, squinting. Under her breath she murmured, "He had his heart set on a ride."

"What about you? Is your heart set on a ride?"

She blushed.

"There's room in the plane for both you and Billy. It holds four people. I told your husband that."

These last words had just slipped out. And Jim was sorry, because Helen's eyes now flashed as she spoke. "William isn't like other people, Mr. Bass. He—"

"Please, there's no need to explain."

"No, I want to. William needs… he needs…"

"Look! There he is."

"Billy!"

The boy had stepped out from behind an old boathouse on the shore.

Helen held out her arms. "Come here," she called.

Billy came slowly, walking with his head down, looking at his feet. Finally he stood before them on the dock. Helen kneeled down. She lifted his chin. "Were you hiding?" He nodded. The salt from tears had dried on his freckled cheeks.

Jim turned toward the plane. He called over his shoulder in a man-to-man voice. "Billy, I'll need some help here before we take off. Are you ready?"

The boy nodded, blinking.

Jim worked the rope free from the post as Billy watched. Then he scooped up the boy. A grin spread over Billy's face as he was carried. With the boy on his arm, Jim stepped from the dock across to the pontoon. It was a bit of a leap. He grabbed the wing strut with his free arm. "Can you open the door, Billy?"

With Billy inside the plane, Jim turned back towards the dock. "How can you resist a free ride?"

Helen stood looking across at him. Her long braid hung over her shoulder. There was a wild look in her eyes. She darted a quick glance in the direction of the house, and William. The tip of her tongue was between her teeth as she thought for a moment. Then she hitched up her green-striped dress, and leapt across.

"Look how little our house is!" cried Billy. He pressed his nose against the plane's side window. "There's Potto! Look, Mom, he's wagging his tail. He sees us!"

Jim was glad for the boy's chatter. And he was very aware of Helen sitting only a few inches away at his side. She was being as quiet as he was. They didn't dare look at each other. They both knew already that it wasn't going to be a free ride. They would have to pay for this moment of closeness. Somehow.

Billy was the only one with an easy mind. Sitting in the seat behind them, his happiness was complete. "There's my school! I wish it was a school day. Then I could wave down at all the kids." He pressed his forehead against the glass. His voice grew worried. "Maybe they won't believe me when I tell them I rode in a plane." He poked his head between his mother and the pilot. "Mom, will you write me a note? Tell my teacher that it's the truth, that I was really up in a plane?"

Helen laughed. "Sweetheart, you don't need to worry about that yet."

"But will you?"

"Yes, I'll write you a note." She was now looking out her side window, as the plane banked to the right. "What a pretty little town we have."

Greenwood lay below. There was the old white church with its tall steeple. And all the beautiful old houses, painted bright colours. The plane continued in its long wide curve. And now below lay a sight that was not so pretty. The hills on the other side of town were hills made of mine tailings, huge grey piles of mine tailings. Helen shook her head.

"What's wrong?" asked Jim, speaking loudly to be heard over the engine's noise.

"Oh, it's just that mining leaves such an ugly mess!" she called back.

"It can't be helped. We need what the mines produce."

"Are you telling me to eat my spinach? That even if I don't like it, it's good for me?"

He grinned over at her. "Yeah, I guess so. I guess I'm a jerk."

Helen nodded, smiling.

The plane levelled off. Billy's arms were now draped around his mother's neck from behind. He pressed his cheek to her cheek. Jim glanced over at them: mother and son. Their profiles were side by side. But their profiles were not alike. And Helen's skin was smooth and tanned, while the boy's face was covered with freckles.

Jim called over, "Where did you get your freckles, Billy?"

The boy twisted his head around to face his mother: "Mom, where did I get my freckles?"

"From God," she answered.

Billy turned to Jim. "I got them from God."

"Billy, you're choking me, honey." Helen loosened his arms from around her neck.

Then Jim leaned over to her. "Maybe I should keep my mouth shut."

A small smile played over Helen's mouth. She looked at him out of the corner of her eye. "Maybe you should."

Jim nodded, grinning. "The lady says that maybe I should."

They surprised the sleeping Potto as they climbed the porch stairs. He'd gotten used to the noise of the plane. And he hadn't heard their voices as they'd walked up the slope. But their tread on the stairs caused the porch to tremble. Potto woke, and lifted his head. His tail thumped.

"Hello, fella." Helen squatted down beside him. She scratched behind his ears. "I think he's getting deaf."

Jim set Billy down from his shoulders. He had carried him all the way up from the dock. The boy had ridden with his arms spread wide, playing airplane.

Then Jim squatted down beside the dog also. He offered his hand to smell. "How old is he?"

"Old!" cried Billy, crowding close. "See? He's got white whiskers, just like Daddy's."

Both Helen and Jim continued to pet the dog. It was almost a way for them to touch each other. They both became aware of this at the same time, and stopped, at the same time.

Billy squeezed between them, kneeling down. "In dog years, Potto's *really* old. Dad says that he's 90."

Potto's tail thumped faster. His tongue hung panting. It didn't matter what they were saying. Whatever it was, they were saying it about him.

Helen now sat back on her heels, looking on with fondness. "Potto is really William's dog." She lifted her gaze to look at Jim. "When I met William, Potto was already four."

Jim was looking at her intently. "How long have you been married?"

"Ten years," Helen answered, forcing her voice to be light. She stood up. "Can I make you lunch? You must be hungry."

"You must have heard my stomach growl."

"Yes I did."

Heaven help me, thought Jim, as he followed Helen into the kitchen. *Heaven help me*. Maybe he was feeling light-headed from no food. Maybe it was simply the presence of this small woman who moved so lightly ahead of him. She was so close that he could smell the fragrance of her hair.

In the kitchen, she knew where everything was. She moved quickly, from the fridge to the stove to the counter. Jim sat at the table with his cap in his hand, watching. He felt as if he was spying on her in her own house.

Helen now pulled out a tray. Sandwich, tea, apple. She placed them on the tray. She was looking around the kitchen: "What have I forgotten?" She opened a drawer, and added a cloth napkin. Then she picked up the tray. "I'll be right back. I'm a little late with William's lunch."

Jim slapped his cap against his knee and started to stand up. "I'm in the way here. I'd better go."

"No, don't move. Sit down, please. William never comes down to lunch. So stay. I mean, unless you want to go. If you want to go, I'll understand. Do you want to?"

"No."

"All right," and she smiled with relief. Then she glanced at Billy, who was standing on a stool at the counter. "Don't touch that knife, honey. I'll be right back and peel your apple."

Billy was sitting across from Jim when Helen returned. On the table in front of Billy sat a peeled apple. The boy was staring at the apple with open pride. "I used his pocketknife, Mom. He showed me how."

Jim looked up at Helen. "I told him that the skin of an apple is good for him."

"I only like the white part," said Billy, still staring at his apple.

"We know that, Billy." Helen gave Jim a look. "He could have cut himself."

Jim kept quiet.

"All right, I know. I'm too protective."

Jim knew better than to agree. He said nothing. But his stomach gave a loud growl.

Helen smiled in spite of herself. "Is that all you have to say?"

"No. There's something I would like to ask you."

"What is it?"

"May I have one of those?" He nodded towards the bowl of fruit on the table.

"Oh dear, I promised you lunch and now I'm starving you." Helen pushed the bowl towards him. "Yes, of course, take anything you want."

Jim reached for an apple. He held it up, turning it this way and that. By now he had gotten Billy's attention. The boy stared across at the bush pilot. He watched as his hero bit into the apple's shiny red skin.

At that moment, a loud BOOM shook the house. Helen yelped and clapped her hand over her mouth. Jim stopped chewing. Another blast rattled the windowpanes. Jim raised his eyebrows in question.

Helen gasped out, "It's only Monty—Monty Reed."

"Only?" said Jim.

"He's a miner. He doesn't usually blast on Sundays, he's not supposed to. But he's been gone. And now I guess he's back."

Jim stared at Helen, at her flushed cheeks. "He must be making up for lost time."

"Yes, I guess so." She pressed her hand to her chest, and laughed. "My heart is beating so fast!"

"May I write to you?"

"What?" Helen's laughter stopped short. Her hand was still pressed to her chest.

In a low voice, Jim repeated himself. "I'd like to know if I can write to you."

"I…" Helen darted a glance at Billy. "I'm… always the one who picks up the mail."

For a long moment they looked at one another.

"Sir?"

They both jumped, startled. Then Jim slowly turned his gaze from Helen's dark eyes. "Yes, Billy?"

"Can I use your pocketknife again? I'm going to cut this apple into little pieces to fit in my mouth."

Crossed Letters

Letters sometimes cross in the mail. Two people who live many miles apart will sit down to write each other at the very same time. They each take up a pen, and a clean sheet of paper, and begin.

As they write, each person is talking to the other in their mind. They tell the news. They ask questions. But most of all they talk about themselves. They tell what they're feeling, and why. Sometimes they blame the other person for how they're feeling, if they're feeling sad. Then they sign their names, and both letters are mailed.

These letters pass each other in the sky, flying in opposite directions. Then they arrive, and are opened, and read. This is when the confusion begins. It's confusing because the questions in one letter are already answered in the other letter.

It's confusing because the person who complained about not getting a letter… now has a letter! And is now happy, not sad—the way it says in the letter the other person is reading at this very moment, and feeling upset, because he *did* write. When letters cross in the mail, it's like two people talking at once.

4

Silver Lake Bed & Breakfast
Rural Route #2
Greenwood, B.C.
May 2, 1988

Dear Jim,

I had given up on getting a letter from you. Many things went through my mind. I won't tell you all of them. But I did feel like a fool some days. I'd walk to the mailbox, and on the way I would tell myself, "Don't get your hopes up, Helen." But I would. For three weeks I opened the mailbox. And for three weeks I walked back to the house with a very heavy heart.

Do you think I'm crazy? Potto does. During those three weeks he always followed me down the driveway. On the way to the mailbox his tail would be wagging. He knew I was hoping for a letter. And on the way back, he'd lick my hand and whimper, pretending that he too was sad.

I think he got confused today. As I shut the mailbox, he started to whine and make sad noises, to comfort me. But then I started spinning around in a circle. I felt like dancing. Poor Potto. He stood there looking at me. His tail moved a little. He wasn't sure.

I sat down on the bank and read your letter aloud to him. He liked it. He liked it a lot.

But then I had to hurry back to the house. We have six guests right now. All three guest rooms are full. So I had to hurry back and make the beds and clean. The guests always want to talk, and it's fun to have them around.

But that day, I just wanted to go off in a corner with your letter and read your words again…

Helen looked up from the letter she was writing. Her gaze drifted towards the window. The guests had gone out for a walk. Billy was in school. William was up in the attic. These facts were at the back of her mind. For the moment she was free. She was free to remember Jim.

She could see the outline of his broad shoulders, his back. And the way he would hitch up his pants. She smiled to herself. She could hear his laugh, and the low quiet voice he used when he talked to Billy.

It was harder to remember his face. It was a broad face. Tanned. With a wide smile. And blue, blue eyes…

"Helen?" William stood in the doorway. "There you are. It's so quiet in the house."

Helen's hand wanted to cover the letter she was writing. She forced her hand not to move.

"Who are you writing to?"

"My brother." The lie had slipped out with ease. It shocked her. She had lied to William.

"Strange—that's the reason I came down. I need you to ask him something."

"Ask my brother?"

"No, no. Not your brother. I want you to ask that fellow to send me a receipt."

"Who? Who do you want a receipt from?"

"That fellow, the one with the plane. I'll need a receipt for my taxes."

Helen's fingers were trembling when she picked up the pen again…

Jim, I just had such a shock. William surprised me a moment ago. He's gone now. He wants you to send him a receipt for the plane ride. My hand is shaking as I write this.

…

It's a little later now. I've just come back from a short walk. I had to get some air. I had to think.

I don't know if we should write to each other. Now I understand what you meant in your letter—that you want to do the right thing. I feel the same way. And I don't want to hurt William.

I also can understand why you waited three weeks to write to me. It's true what you said: once we start writing to each other, how will we stop?

But wait a minute! We're being silly. There's no reason to stop, if we're just friends. Let's agree to that, okay? Let's be friends. There's nothing wrong with two friends writing to each other. I'll tell you about my life here, and you can tell me about all your adventures — oh! Do you see where my pen skipped? I have to catch my breath. We just had another underground blast from our miner. He's been very busy lately.

From your letter, it sounds like you're not home very much. You seem to be always flying off somewhere. It must have been wonderful to have your wife go with you on your trips. And it must have been very hard to lose her to a drunk driver. I hope he was punished.

But of course that doesn't bring back your wife. From what you say, you must have had a perfect life with her. How could anyone take her place?

I have to go. I can hear the guests coming up the porch stairs. Remember the receipt. I have to go, good-bye.

Your friend,
Helen

May 12

Dear Jim,

I'll tell you my first thought when I opened the mailbox and saw your letter: "How does Jim know it's my birthday?"

But of course you couldn't have known, since I never told you.

Shall I tell you my age? Most women keep their age a secret. But I've always wanted to be older, to be wise. I spotted my first grey hair the other morning. I was very excited, and I ran to show Billy. He looked up at me and his eyes filled with tears. He wants me to have black hair always and forever. Billy doesn't like change.

Once I was cutting his hair in front of the mirror. And I looked up at myself and said out loud, "I wonder what I would look like with short hair." Well, Billy grabbed the scissors from my hand. "No, Mom!" He stared into the mirror at me. His face was so fierce. I love him so much.

Do you remember asking him where he got his freckles? Of course I know the reason that you asked. Billy looks nothing like me, or even William.

The fact is, William and I were never able to have a child of our own. And then I heard about Billy. He was already two years old when we adopted him. But that was fine with William, because he didn't really want an infant. You know—crying all the time.

Your letter was postmarked from Calgary. I wonder when you will be back, and read this.

None of the guests are awake yet. It's only five in the morning. I'm writing this out on the porch. I couldn't sleep. It gets light so early now. But rain is dripping off the edge of the roof. I have to go in soon and start breakfast for nine people. What do you eat for breakfast? Do you eat the same thing every day, like most men?

Yes, I miss you. Does that answer your question?

William asked me if I'd written to you about the receipt. I told him yes.

May 19

Dearest Jim,

Yes, it's the same for me, I miss you terribly. It's raining again here. It's been raining for days. Terrible weather for the guests. One family left early. But the lovebirds on their honeymoon are still here. They leave today. The truth is that I'll be glad when they're gone. I'm always coming around the corner and finding them locked in an embrace. It confuses me so much. I guess I envy them.

Oh Jim—what are we going to do? Yes, I want to see you, but when? How?

No, I'll never cut my hair, if you don't want me to. You say you want my promise on it—so I promise.

The mail truck has already gone past today, so this letter won't go out until tomorrow. And then it's the weekend, and then a holiday—Victoria Day. I hate holidays, I hate weekends, I hate every day that's not a mail day.

I guess it's the rain that's getting me down. And William is not happy. He suffers so much. He's been trying to paint the waterfall. And I know that his work can't be going very well, because he won't talk.

At least the daily blasting from Monty Reed has stopped. His license has been suspended for three months. William went to the RCMP to complain about the Sunday blasting, which is against the law. He came back looking very pleased with himself.

I admit that when I saw William come in with a smile on his face my heart lifted. It was like having the rain stop and the sun come out. I asked him if he wanted a cup of tea. He said yes, and I fixed it the way that he likes it. But he didn't stay, he took the cup with him up to the attic.

It was just a little thing. I sat there at the table for a long time. If only he had just sat down with me for a minute, and talked…

It was time for Billy's bedtime story. Helen sat on the edge of his bed. "What story would you like tonight, sweetheart?" It was a silly question. Helen knew exactly which story Billy wanted to hear.

At every bedtime, his freckled face looked up eagerly from the pillow. And once again, Helen would relate the adventures of the White Dragonfly.

Like all her stories, she made it up as she went along. Of course, it would have to have a happy ending. All children insist on happy endings, or else they can't sleep.

By now the Dragonfly had found a mate. His mate was just like him—all white. They flew side by side, their white wings trembling. They were always together. They flew low over the lake.

They hovered above lily pads. They darted here and there as they hunted for insects to eat. They flew fast, and with their huge eyes they saw everything.

"Do they see me?"

"Oh yes, they see you, Billy."

"But they don't want to eat me—no." And his head wagged back and forth on the pillow.

"I'm not sure. Let's see how you taste." Helen lifted Billy's freckled arm to her mouth. Baring her teeth she pretended to nibble on his skin. Then she spit him out—"Yuk!"—while Billy's laughter rang loud.

William's voice cut through their laughter. "I lost track of the time."

Helen turned her head to look at him. He stood in the doorway of Billy's bedroom. "You didn't call me to supper," he added.

"Your plate is in the fridge, William. You know that you hate to be disturbed when you're painting."

"Yes, yes of course. The time slipped by me." He looked at the two of them together, Helen sitting on the edge of Billy's bed. His voice when he spoke was almost wistful. "What's the story tonight?"

"It's about a dragonfly," Helen answered quickly.

"Two dragonflies!" cried Billy.

"Oh? And what do these two dragonflies do?"

"It's late." Helen bent down to Billy and kissed him. "Goodnight."

William called his goodnight from the doorway.

But Billy couldn't answer. His lips were sealed with that kiss. Instead he waved. And William waved back before turning out the light and closing the door.

That night Helen waited until she could be sure that William was asleep. Then she crept into their bedroom. Quietly she stepped up on the little stool and climbed into the high bed.

She had told William to go to bed without her. Her excuse was that the stove needed cleaning, and that she wouldn't have time in the morning. The bed-and-breakfast was empty of guests, but William knew that more guests were due. So he didn't suspect anything.

Helen lay without touching her husband. She lay on her back, and stared up into the dark. What would it be like to be lying beside Jim. *Oh god, forgive me*. She covered her face with her hands.

She was still awake at 1:00 a.m. when an explosion flashed at the window—KAH-BOOM!

William jumped straight out of bed and stood swaying on his feet. "It's Monty!" he gasped.

The explosion had ripped across Helen's thoughts. It had caught her thinking of Jim. She felt dazed, and guilty, caught in the act. Her body was shaking all over from the loudness of the blast. Her ears rang.

She sat up. With shaking fingers she reached out, and turned on the bedside lamp. The light caught William in his nightshirt, standing in the middle of the room. His white hair hung wildly from his head. He too was shaking all over. And his fear was turning to rage. His face was pale, "I'll kill him!"

Helen's heart skipped a beat. For a moment she thought he meant Jim. He was going to kill Jim.

William's voice was low and deadly. "Monty will pay for this."

"No, William." Helen climbed down from the high bed. At the window, she peered out into the darkness. "The explosion wasn't underground. I saw the flash. It was down by the main road." She turned to William. "Down at the end of our driveway."

They looked at each other.

"The mailbox," William whispered. A strange smile spread slowly across his face. "Where's the flashlight?" He was putting on his slippers.

"The flashlight is where it always is—in the kitchen drawer." She stared after him. Suddenly she remembered: her letter to Jim was still in the mailbox. She had walked down after supper with the letter.

For a long moment Helen couldn't move. *Maybe William has blown up the mailbox himself. Maybe he already knows about my letters to Jim. Maybe he was only pretending when he blamed Monty for the blast.*

Her own thoughts shocked her. Reason returned. William had been up in the attic all afternoon and evening. *But he could have used a timer on the bomb.*

"Wait!" she called, "I'm coming too."

She ran down the porch steps in her nightgown. She was barefoot. She ran after William. The driveway was muddy under her feet. But the rain had stopped. Stars were appearing overhead.

"William! Where are you going? Can't it wait until morning?"

William didn't answer, or slow down. He strode on long legs down the driveway. The flashlight's circle of light bobbed ahead of him.

All Helen needed was a little time. What if the mailbox were still standing? What if William opened the box and shone the flashlight in and found her letter to Jim?

Helen caught up to William at the bottom of the drive. The flashlight beamed down on a twisted piece of metal. And here was another piece. It was part of the mailbox. Helen could read "TURN…" on one of the shards of metal. The name "TURNER" had been torn apart.

William shifted the flashlight's beam to where the mailbox had stood. The only thing left standing was the steel post set in concrete. But it was only a post. The mailbox itself was gone. And the wooden platform that it had sat upon was blasted to splinters.

The night was silent, except for the croak of frogs along the ditch. In the air was a strange smell from the explosion. William sniffed, and nodded slowly in recognition. "Black powder," he said with satisfaction.

To Helen, William seemed strangely calm, almost happy. She stepped away from him. "Ow!" She had stepped on something. "Ow! William—shine the flashlight over here."

It was glass. In the mud and gravel of the road she had stepped on broken glass. Another piece of glass shone under the flashlight's beam. And another.

"Helen! Where are your slippers? Don't move." William picked his way through the pieces of twisted metal scattered along the driveway. "How could you be so foolish as to come out here barefoot!" He leaned down. "Your foot is bleeding. Here, put your arms around my neck." And he lifted her up.

Helen's mind whirled. She held on to William. She clung with her arms around his neck as he carried her up the driveway. He still had the flashlight in one hand. The light bobbed crazily ahead of them.

"You can put me down now, I'm sure it's safe, there's no glass here."

"No, you're bleeding."

Helen watched the light dance along the gravel and mud of the driveway. It felt so strange to be carried in William's arms, to be held so close. How could she have imagined such terrible things about him? Maybe he loved her, after all. What was he thinking, right now, as he carried her?

"This is Monty's doing. He has a grudge against me, because I reported him. It's because of me that his license is suspended. So this is his thank-you card—a bomb. But for once he's going to pay. He won't get away with this, I promise you, Helen."

"Put me down."

"You're very light. It's no trouble."

"Put me down."

William stopped, "Very well." But even as he opened his arms,

Helen leapt to the ground. She ran ahead, up the driveway. Her long nightgown caught at her legs as she ran.

"Helen, your foot is cut!"

But she knew the road. And she knew where she was going. The lawn was cold and wet under her bare feet as she ran down the slope to the dock. The lake was dark. As she walked out, it lapped quietly against the posts.

She walked out to the very end of the dock and sat down. She drew her legs up under her nightgown and bowed her head to her knees. She listened to her heart pounding. Her marriage was over. As quietly as she could, as quietly as the water lapping at the posts, she let the sobs come.

William shouted from the porch: "Helen, are you coming in?" She made no reply. Her head still rested on her knees. What was she going to do? She drew a long sigh. Her foot was throbbing.

Then a thought darted across her mind. She lifted her head. The mailbox had been blown apart. But what about the broken glass? The mailbox had been made of metal. So where had the glass come from?

"Sorry to bother you so early in the morning, Mrs. Turner."

The corporal's voice startled Helen. She stepped out of the toolshed. She held a rake in one hand.

It was only 6:00 a.m. Helen intended to rake up the glass at the bottom of the driveway. To Corporal Jupp she said, "Our mailbox was blown up last night."

He tipped his cap. "Correct, Mrs. Turner."

Helen glanced over at the RCMP car. Another Mountie sat inside. She turned back to the corporal. "Then you must have heard the explosion."

The Mountie's face reddened. "Not exactly. We got a report about a missing person. Somebody who didn't come home after the pub closed."

Helen gripped the rake with both hands. "What do you mean? What does that have to do with our mailbox getting blown apart?"

"Mrs. Turner, we'd like to know if you or your husband heard anything unusual last night, before the bomb went off."

"So it *was* a bomb."

"A very powerful bomb. Is your husband here? We'd like to talk to him." Corporal Jupp looked towards the house.

Helen followed his gaze. "No," she shook her head. "I mean, yes, he's here, but he's not awake yet. He had a bad night." She stepped to go around the Mountie with her rake. "I have to go clean up the mess. We have guests coming later this morning."

"I don't think you understand, Mrs. Turner." All flirtation was gone from the Mountie's voice. "There was an attempt on someone's life last night."

"You mean *murder*?"

"Monty Reed is a very lucky man. The bomb blew the floorboards up through the cab of his pickup."

"Monty *Reed*?"

Corporal Jupp turned to greet William. "Mr. Turner, good morning. We're sorry to get you up so early."

William was coming up the slope towards the toolshed. He

wore a striped robe over his nightshirt. When he reached the corporal he shook his hand. "It's good to know that the RCMP is so quick on the job. Someone blew up our mailbox last night, and I know who did it."

"I'm afraid that this is a case of attempted murder, sir. A man is in hospital. We believe you know him. His name is Monty Reed."

The effect of the Mountie's words on William was startling. His face paled. He began to tremble and perspire. He looked down at the ground, and whispered the name of his enemy. "Monty." Then he lifted his head, and squinted at Corporal Jupp. "I… I suppose he will live?"

"Oh, he's just cut up a bit. A very lucky man. Someone strapped a bomb under the cab of his pickup. The device must have been on a timer. It blew up just as Mr. Reed was heading home past your driveway."

William slowly shook his head in disbelief.

"The explosion happened shortly after 1:00 a.m."

William looked around for Helen. He reached out blindly.

But Helen had stepped back from the circle of men. She still held the rake in her grip. She looked off towards the lake as she listened to the corporal.

"Monty Reed had been at the pub, Mr. Turner. He was at the pub from seven last night until it closed at one in the morning. During that time, his pickup was parked out in front. We believe the bomb was planted during those six hours. Now, we know there are some squabbles between the miners in town, over mining claims and so on. The bombing may have something to do with that."

As the Mountie spoke, William tried to keep a straight face. But a smile played about his mouth. He cupped his hand over his chin and mouth, to appear serious.

"It seems that Mr. Reed had no kind words for you, Mr. Turner. We understand that he spoke against you in a very loud voice. A voice loud enough to be heard by everyone in the pub."

William laughed. "You don't think that *I* did it!"

By now the other Mountie had gotten out of the car and joined them.

"No, Mr. Turner. We just want to know if you saw or heard anything unusual last night."

"What I heard was an explosion. It threw me out of bed."

As the two Mounties spoke with William, Helen backed away. Then she turned and walked swiftly down the driveway with her rake. She tried to make herself seem as small as possible, so that no one would notice her departure.

In daylight, the scene of the bombing looked like a war zone. The trees around the explosion had lost most of their leaves in the blast. And the ground was littered with shards of metal and wood. There still remained a faint smell of the explosive in the air.

And of course the ground sparkled with crystals of broken glass. The glass was everywhere, blown from the pickup's windshield. Glass in the weeds, glass across the driveway, glass out on the pavement of the main road. The sharp pieces glittered in the early morning sun.

Yes, it was a beautiful morning. Yes, the spring rains had finally stopped. But Helen had other things on her mind. She began to rake up the glass and bits of metal from the mailbox. Where was her letter to Jim? It must have been torn into pieces along with the mailbox. But how big were the pieces?

As Helen raked, she searched for scraps of paper. And she found them, here and there. The scraps of her letter looked like flakes of snow, but they didn't melt in the warm sunshine.

Helen kept raking. What had she written to Jim in the letter? She couldn't remember. *Here!* She bent down and picked up a scrap of paper. She read the words aloud: "…cut my hair."

She stared at the scrap of sentence. The sentence had been torn apart. What she had promised Jim was that she would never cut her hair.

She looked about her. It was as if her life lay scattered in pieces on the driveway.

She tore the scrap of writing into even smaller bits. No one could read it now. Then she began to rake as fast as she could.

She was still raking when the blue and white patrol car came slowly drown the driveway behind her. The corporal didn't honk. He leaned his head out the window, "Excuse us, Mrs. Turner."

Helen stood to one side with her rake, to let the Mounties pass.

Instead the car stopped beside her, with the engine running. "Don't want to get a flat tire."

Helen nodded.

The two men inside the car were silent for a moment, looking at her. Then the other Mountie leaned across in front of the corporal: "Did you see the pickup, Mrs. Turner?" And he pointed. "It went over the bank down there. And you can see the hole in the pavement from the bomb."

Helen nodded again. The two men in the car were still looking at her with interest. Finally the younger Mountie spoke again. "Looks like a nice day."

"Yes," Helen agreed. *What do they want? Why aren't they going away?* Then she realized: they were flirting with her!

Yet she had no lipstick on. And her hair—her hand flew to her head. She had brushed her hair this morning, but in her rush she had forgotten to braid it. It hung down around her shoulders and arms, dark and thick. She felt suddenly exposed to these men. She stepped back. Her heels were at the edge of the ditch. "It's safe to pass now. I raked it clear."

The Mounties tipped their caps. Slowly, they did as they were told—drove on.

When Helen returned to the house, William was sitting at the kitchen table. He had a Sears catalog open in front of him. "Here, Helen. This one." His finger rested on the page. It was a picture of a white mailbox. The deluxe model, very large. The cost was $69.95, plus tax.

But Helen gave only a brief glance at the page. "William, I need your help."

He was still looking at the page in the catalog. "We needed a bigger mailbox anyway." He looked up with a smile. "So whoever bombed Monty's pickup did us a favor."

"William, it's still a mess down there. And I haven't made up the beds for the new guests yet."

"What about getting that teenager?" he asked cheerfully. "The boy who helped last time."

"You mean Rex."

"Yes. First he can clean up the mess to your satisfaction. Then I want him to build a wooden platform for the new mailbox to sit on." He turned his attention back to the page in the catalog. He checked the figures. "Tell him to build it 24 inches long, and nine inches wide."

Then William stood up from the table. He rubbed his hands together with glee. "And tell him… tell him we're going to need a boulder. We'll put a boulder right next to the steel post. Then if someone runs off the road, they'll run into the boulder, and not our mailbox!" He was smiling down at Helen. "What is it? Can't I be happy? You know that I would never wish anyone harm. But there's nothing wrong in Monty Reed getting a little of his own medicine. Don't you agree?"

He didn't notice. He didn't have any idea that everything had changed for her. She was married to a man she no longer loved. And he didn't know it.

And here was Billy, yawning as he wandered into the kitchen. "Mom, I had a strange dream last night."

Helen poured cereal into his bowl. "Was there a loud boom in your dream?"

A smile cracked his sleepy face. "Yeah. Hey, how did you know?"

She poured milk over his cereal. "Eat up. Then you can get ready for school. I'll drive you today." She didn't look at William as she added, "I have to go into town."

Potto followed Helen out to the car. He didn't like rain. For the last week he had slept under the kitchen table as the rain poured down outside. But today was dry and sunny, just his kind of day.

"Potto? Are you coming too?" Helen opened the door for him. He climbed in slowly. He took his place on the front seat.

"Billy? Come on, sweetheart. Potto, you're going to have to move over to the middle of the seat. Billy's coming too."

Potto didn't move. This was his favorite place to ride, by the window. He could poke his nose into the breeze as they drove along.

"Billy, can you sit in the middle this time?… That's great. All right, we're off." Helen started the car. The guests wouldn't arrive before 10:00 a.m.

"Mom, do you know what happened in my dream last night? Mom? Are you listening?"

"What is it, Billy?"

"In my dream there was a big old crow. He was flying around Potto's dish, he was trying to get his dog food. And then it wasn't a crow anymore, it turned into an airplane. This black plane was flying around, and all of a sudden, Bang!—somebody shot it."

"No!" Helen reached out for Billy's leg as she drove. "Don't say that. Never say that, Billy."

"What's wrong? What did I say?"

"I'm sorry, never mind." Helen patted his knee. "You just scared me." She parked in front of the school.

"Don't worry, Mom. It wasn't the Dragonfly. It didn't have those float things underneath."

Helen blushed. So he knew. She turned to look at him. "I'm glad, Billy." Then she smiled. "Do you think I'm silly?"

"Yup," he nodded. He let her kiss his head. But he didn't move. "Mom?"

"Yes, Billy?"

"I have to get out on your side."

"Oh! Of course you do. I must have been daydreaming. Potto, you stay here."

Whack-whack.

"Yes, you guard the car like a good dog."

The sidewalk in front of the school was crowded with kids of all ages. "Billy, honey, I have to talk to that young man. Rex. Do you know where I might find him?"

Helen followed her son along the sidewalk and around the corner. Then Billy pointed. "That's where they smoke."

A group of teenagers leaned against the wall in the morning sun. Clouds of smoke hovered around their heads. "There he is," said Billy, pointing.

"Yes, I see him." But Helen didn't move forward.

"Mom?"

"Yes, Billy."

"I think maybe you forgot to make my lunch." He squinted up at her.

"Billy, you're right, I forgot. It's been such a busy morning. I haven't even had time to look in the mirror." Or braid her hair. It still hung long around her shoulders and arms.

"Billy, I'll bring your lunch in at noon," she called after him. Then her head turned at the sound of a wolf whistle.

The whistle had come from the group of teenagers leaning against the wall. Helen took a deep breath, and walked towards them.

"Rex?"

"Oh hi, Mrs. Turner." Leaning against the wall, Rex blew smoke from his mouth. And grinned. "Hey, your hair looks nice like that."

$\mathcal{R}$ed Flag

When the red flag is raised on the side of a mailbox, it's a signal that a letter is waiting inside to be mailed. It tells the mail truck to stop.

The small red flag is easily seen from a distance. It looks almost like a red flower on a red stalk. But the flag is made of metal. It stands securely in its slot. In a wind, the red flag doesn't rattle against the side of the mailbox. It doesn't bend, as a flower would bend. It remains upright and firm, like some decisions. It's a signal to the mail truck and anyone driving by that something is up.

5

It had been two months since Jim Bass had flown William to see the waterfall. It had been the same two long months since the pilot had sat at the kitchen table and asked Helen, "May I write to you?"

But today there had been no letter from Jim at the post office. There had only been bills and a catalog for William. And a large parcel. Helen carried the parcel into the kitchen. She was surprised to see William there, pacing back and forth.

He turned to her and announced. "I can't paint, Helen. I can't paint, and I may never paint again."

She set the parcel on the kitchen counter.

He had been like this for days. It was a relief for Helen to get out of the house, even for short trips to the post office to pick up their mail.

"It's the waterfall, Helen. It's fighting me. I'll never be able to finish that painting. I know it."

Helen knew that whatever she said would be turned against her. She got the knife from the drawer. She began cutting through the tape on the parcel.

"What's that?"

"The new mailbox from Sears."

"Let me do it." He took the knife from her hand. In a few moments, the new mailbox was lifted out. It was just what he had ordered. It was large and white and shiny. "Good," he nodded. "Perfect. And worth every penny."

An hour later Helen heard his steps coming down from the attic. She heard him call her name.

"I'm in here, William. In the laundry room." She was stuffing sheets into the washing machine.

William appeared at the doorway. He held up the new white mailbox and spoke with pride. "The paint is not quite dry on the lettering." And he looked again at the black lettering printed on the side of the mailbox. He had taken a great deal of care with it. It read, "WILLIAM TURNER" in perfect black letters.

Helen poured soap into the washing machine. She slammed down the lid. "Where's my name?"

"What do you mean?"

"You have your name painted on there, but where's mine? We both live here."

"But you're my wife!"

Helen spoke slowly, "Yes… that's true."

"You're *Mrs.* William Turner. Everyone knows that. I don't need to put it on the mailbox. Besides, this is exactly the same as what was on our old mailbox."

"You're wrong there."

"How am I wrong?"

Helen turned the knob of the washing machine. A hum filled the small room. Then she looked up at him. "Our old mailbox read, 'William Turner, Silver Lake Bed & Breakfast.'"

William studied the mailbox and its perfect lettering. "You're right. Helen, you're right. Wait—don't go yet." He rested the heavy mailbox on the edge of the dryer. He cleared his throat. He swallowed. "I'll change it."

The washing machine switched to the next cycle. A louder cycle. William spoke over the noise of the machine. He pointed, "And right here I'll add 'Mr. & Mrs.'"

"I don't care." She turned to go.

"Wait, Helen. I said I'll change it."

But she was already walking down the hall. She called over her shoulder, "I don't care what's on the mailbox."

Rex was on the job. He lifted up the heavy iron bar, then plunged it into the dirt, where it stood upright. Then he took a rest. He wiped his forehead, and gulped a swig of his beer. He hid the bottle back among the weeds on top of the bank.

He grabbed the iron bar again, and rocked it back and forth against the rock. The rock still wouldn't budge. It was huge, a boulder, and it was set firmly into the side of the bank.

It was Rex's job to work it free.

The sun was hot. The job was a dirty one. His bare legs were covered with dust. Once more he angled the bar under the rock. He tried to move it, failed, and took another rest.

"Is it out yet?" called William. He was walking down the driveway. He'd gone back to the house to get his sun hat. Besides the hat, he wore a long-sleeved shirt with the collar turned up at the neck. His pale skin couldn't bear the sun's rays. In fact, he should have worn gloves. William looked down at his wrists. They were already turning red from sunburn. He'd been out here almost an hour, keeping an eye on the boy.

"I think that you might use the shovel now," he said to Rex. William stood over the boy as he dug around the boulder. The huge rock was perfect for William's purpose. "Now take the bar and pry at the top."

William moved to the shade, but kept a sharp eye on Rex. The boy wore only a pair of cutoff jeans. But he was young. And the young defy even the sun's power. They think that nothing can hurt them. They think that they will never get old.

"Yes! That's it," shouted William. He hurried from the shade to stand behind Rex. "Push!"

The boy pushed on the bar. The rock was being angled free of the soil's grip. "Keep at it, boy, keep at it…"

But the rock fell back against the bank.

"Why did you give up?" cried William.

"It's a heavy rock, Mr. Turner."

"Of course it's a heavy rock. It's a boulder! Now… try again."

Rex darted a longing glance towards the weeds above the bank. He licked his lips. It was hot. He was thirsty.

"Try again," urged William.

It was an hour before the boulder was in place. It now leaned snug against the post for the mailbox. Rex had rolled the huge rock turn by turn across the driveway. He now straightened up. Sweat dripped from beneath his short curly hair.

"Look at this," called William from over by the bank. His voice was filled with disgust. He reached up for the bottle of beer hidden in the weeds. "Teenagers start drinking, they drive by and throw their bottles and cans out the window. They think that the world is their garbage can."

Rex walked over. "That's mine," he said in a tight voice.

"Yours? This is your beer? Well, there will be no drinking on the job."

And William poured out the rest of the beer as the boy watched with narrowed eyes. He watched as William walked over to the green Camaro and set the empty bottle on the fender.

"Now…" said William, dusting off his hands. He smiled over at Rex.

Rex was not smiling. His face was grim. His dark brows were knit in an angry frown.

"Come up to the house, young man. My wife will pay you your wage. It's a job well done." William turned to look back at their work. The boulder was in place. He smiled with grim satisfaction. Aloud, he declared, "No one will dare touch *that* mailbox."

Rex muttered under his breath.

"Did you say something?" asked William. But he was staring at the new white mailbox on its post. The mailbox gleamed in the sun. A red metal flag lay in a slot along one side. And on the other side, in perfect black letters, was printed:

WILLIAM TURNER
SILVER LAKE BED & BREAKFAST

As soon as William's back was turned, Rex grabbed the beer bottle off the fender. He weighed it his hand. His teeth were clenched. But he didn't throw the bottle at the back of William's head. There was a better way to get even.

That same afternoon, Helen was in the garden when she heard the cry from William. She'd been weeding for hours. To be cooler, she'd pinned her braid in a circle on top of her head. And now the sun was beating down on the bare nape of her neck.

At the cry, she looked up. It was a cry of victory. The attic window flew open. William leaned out. "Helen! I've finished!"

William has finished his painting. Helen's stomach clenched. She knew what that meant. For weeks he had given all his time to that square of canvas. All his hours had been spent up in the attic.

"Helen! Come on up!"

She threw her handful of weeds onto the pile. Slowly she stood up, and brushed dirt from her knees. The knot was still in her stomach.

William met her at the bottom of the attic stairs. He held the door open. His face was flushed pink. "Helen, I came in from moving that boulder with the boy, and I felt so much energy! So I came up here. And now it's done—in the last two hours!"

With a slow step, Helen followed William up the narrow stairs to the attic. She felt as if her feet were made of lead. William never let her see a painting of his before it was finished. And now it was finished. *The Waterfall*. She stood before the canvas. She could feel William staring at her.

"What do you think?"

Helen could hardly breathe in the hot attic. And her stomach felt tight. She stared at the painting for a long moment. Then she turned to William. His face was so open, so eager. This what he lived for. Painting. This is what he had spent the last two months working on.

Helen couldn't lie to him. She spoke in a level voice. "It's very good, William. I think it's the best painting you've ever done."

There was a moment's pause. What Helen had longed for only two months ago, she now dreaded. William stepped forward and caught her up. He lifted her in his arms and kissed her, hard. She tried to turn her head away. He kissed her ear, her neck.

"Stop!" Helen twisted away, "Put me down!" Her own words shocked her. She was panting with anger. "This is what you always do! You ignore me for months. And then you paw me like an animal—just because you have a painting to sell!"

William stepped back. His face filled with horror at her anger. His white hair was mussed from their struggle. It hung down over his eyes.

"And look! You've got paint on me!" she cried. She tried to rub it off her arms. She couldn't look at him now. Her cheeks burned. For now she *was* lying.

In her heart she knew the real reason that she'd pushed William away. It wasn't only because he'd neglected her for the last two months. The real reason, the deeper reason, was that she no longer loved him. She no longer welcomed his kiss, or his touch. She'd pushed William away because she didn't want him. She wanted Jim.

William now dared a step towards her. "Helen, I'm sorry! I had no idea that you felt like this."

"Didn't you?" She still couldn't look at him. Instead she turned towards the painting, though not really seeing it.

William dared another step closer to his wife. "No, I didn't…" And then he couldn't help it, he stole a glance at his painting. He couldn't pull his eyes away. A smile crept around his mouth. He stared, openly. He had done it! He had captured the waterfall!

Helen caught him. She caught the look on his face as he stared at his own creation. It was a look of wonder.

A giggle rose in her throat. She started to laugh. "Oh William, William…" She shook her head and her wild laughter filled the attic.

"What? What is it? Why are you laughing?"

"I'm laughing because…" And she tried to catch her breath. She had started to hiccup. "Because I feel free!"

"What do you mean, 'free'? Free of what?"

She shrugged her shoulders. "Just… free." Another hiccup jerked her, and another. But she didn't seem to notice. She just stood there smiling. Laughter had washed all her anger away, and all her guilt. The hiccups continued to jerk her narrow shoulders.

"Helen, you must go drink a large glass of water," said William.

He put his hands on her shoulders and steered her down the stairs.

At the bottom of the stairs they met a guest coming out of the hall bathroom. The guest looked at Helen with concern: "My advice is to hold your breath for 10 seconds. That always cures my hiccups."

In the morning, William knocked at the door of the spare bedroom. "Helen? Are you awake?" Helen sometimes slept apart from William if she had a headache. William waited. It was very early. He slowly opened the door. "Are you feeling better?"

Helen sat crouched on the window seat in her nightgown. From the window she had been watching the sunrise.

She turned her gaze from the window. "I feel fine," she said, her voice calm. It had been William's notion that she'd had a headache. She had made no such excuse last night. She'd simply announced that she was going to sleep in the spare room. William had made no protest—though he'd put on a sad face.

This was no sad face looking down at her now. It was a face flushed with excitement. "I'm taking the painting to Spokane, Helen. I'm taking it to my dealer. I don't want to ship it. And I want to see the look on his face when he opens the crate and sees *The Waterfall*."

"But William, how will you get to Spokane? I can't drive you. I'm needed here. The guests don't check out until noon."

"I've decided to drive down myself." There was a touch of both pride and anxiety in William's voice. He didn't like to drive. And he wasn't a good driver. He was far too nervous. He always hunched over the steering wheel, tense. "I'll be back tomorrow afternoon. You don't mind, do you?"

"No, I don't mind," said Helen, as he bent down. He pressed a small kiss to her forehead. It was all he dared.

From the window seat she watched him go. "Drive safely," she called after him. His eagerness touched her. But that was all. She felt nothing else.

The guests were taking a last walk down by the lake before leaving. Their sheets were already in the washing machine. Helen turned on the dryer, which was loaded with wet towels. The two machines filled the laundry room with their noise.

Helen kneeled on the floor, sorting a pile of dirty clothes. She was glad for the work. She needed to keep busy. She felt relieved that William had left for Spokane. But soon he would be back. And he would want her affection. He would want her to...

And then Helen's heart jumped. She raised her head from the pile of dirty clothes. Jim Bass stood in the doorway of the laundry room.

"I knocked, but I guess you couldn't hear."

The sight of his deep blue eyes took her breath away. "Jim." And then a sob rose in her throat. She tried to choke it down.

"Helen—"

"I'll be fine. I'm fine." She got to her feet. He seemed so far away. She stepped over the pile of dirty clothes. She reached out and gripped his plaid shirt in her fists.

He leaned his mouth down on the top of her head. "You're crying," he murmured into her hair. "Does that mean that you're glad to see me?"

She nodded against his chest. His arms were around her now. "Where's William?"

She sniffed, and turned her head to one side. "He won't be back until tomorrow. He took his painting to Spokane."

"Oh. So he finished."

"Yes!" The word was like a wail. Fresh tears welled up. Again she pressed her face into his shirt, as if to hide. "But I couldn't, Jim. I couldn't!"

"You couldn't," he repeated. He didn't understand. But it didn't seem to matter.

Potto was at the doorway. In his mouth he clutched the handle of the toilet brush. He waited cheerfully, his tail wagging.

Helen tilted her head back. Her eyes were shiny with tears. "You're really here."

Jim ran a hand through his wavy brown hair. He seemed a little embarrassed. "Well, I didn't get a letter from you last week. So I thought that I would just show up."

Helen stepped back. She tried to smooth out the wrinkles she had made in his shirt. "I got you all wet."

Jim took a nervous swallow. "Maybe I shouldn't have come."

Helen turned her head away. She spoke in a low voice. "I was too sad to write you."

"What were you sad about—what happened? Is Billy all right?"

"Billy's fine," said Helen, wiping at her tears. Then she nodded towards Potto. "You'd better accept the toilet brush."

"How long will he wait there like that?"

Helen laughed. "Forever."

"Thank you, Potto." Jim held the toilet brush in his hand. "What shall I do with this thing?"

"Well, the toilets need scrubbing," said Helen. Her gay laugh was drowned by the whine of the dryer and the thump-thump of the washing machine.

"Helen, before I scrub the toilets…" Jim's blue eyes grew serious. "Say, can't we turn off those machines for a minute?"

"Why don't we just go into the kitchen?"

"No—not yet."

"Is there something you want to ask me?"

They stood several feet apart. Jim's face was now growing flushed. He looked down at his shoes.

"Mrs. Turner?" It was the voice of one of the guests. "We're leaving now."

"All right," Helen called. "I'll be right out." Then she moved towards Jim. She grabbed his shirt and stood on her tiptoes. "Yes," she whispered, "my answer is 'Yes.' "

The kiss was stolen from the moment. It didn't last long. But Jim Bass knew enough to know that it's always women who make the important decisions.

"I'm coming," Helen called. And she left him leaning against the dryer.

The guests had left. William was still in Spokane. Billy was at school. And Helen and Jim were out on the lake.

The canoe slipped through the water. Jim Bass dipped his paddle in at the stern. He tried to match his stroke to Helen's. She sat up at the prow. She was wearing a white T-shirt and shorts. A single black braid hung down her back. He couldn't take his eyes off her.

Their strokes were now matched perfectly, and the canoe skimmed along.

"How did you learn to tell time by the sun?"

"It's due to William," she called over her shoulder. "He hates to have clocks in the house. But we have a sundial in the garden."

"Let's test your skill. What time is it right now?" Jim glanced at his wristwatch.

Helen tipped her face to the sun. She studied the sun's height above the mountain. "It's almost 11."

"You're very close. It's five minutes after."

The sun shone down. The lake was like a silver mirror as they paddled. It was Jim who finally asked the question that hung in the air.

"Helen, when do you have to be back?"

"Billy gets dropped off by the school bus at 2:30."

They paddled on in silence. There was an excited hum between them. It matched the hum of the insects that flitted over the water. Jim was watching the movement of Helen's shoulders and arms.

Helen was aware of his eyes on her. But then something caught her attention up ahead. "Look!" She lifted her paddle from the water and rested it across the prow.

Ahead, dragonflies hovered over lily pads. The lily pads were dark green. White flowers floated at their centers. The dragonflies whirred about on blue-green wings.

The canoe glided past.

And then Jim saw them: two dragonflies, locked together on a lily pad. They were mating. Together, their two bodies bent to the shape of a heart. Jim held his breath. Helen's face was now in profile to him. For she had seen them too. Jim watched the colour rise from her throat to her cheeks. Then she turned away, and dug her paddle in.

"Where are we going?" he laughed. "And in such a hurry!"

"Don't tease!" she sang back at him.

Just those words, and the way she tossed her head, made Jim's heart contract. He watched her slim, strong arms flash in the sunlight. It was now Helen who was steering the canoe.

They rounded a grassy bank along the shore. Around the other side was a cove. Helen steered them into the cove. Then she lifted up her paddle as the canoe glided through a floating garden of lily pads. And Jim did the same, he lifted out his paddle. The canoe was surrounded. They were enclosed in a world of beauty and stillness.

The prow of the canoe scraped onto the sand. Helen leapt lightly out and steadied the canoe as Jim crept forward. He grabbed the bag of oranges that was their lunch.

On the shore they stood apart from each other, suddenly shy.

They looked out across the water, across the floating lily pads. They were alone on the lake. The white floatplane was so far away that it looked like a tiny toy by a tiny dock.

Without speaking, Jim pointed towards the grassy bank. Helen nodded. She climbed the bank ahead of him, and pushed her way through a screen of bushes. There she sat down, on soft green moss and short grass. Tiny wildflowers were speckled everywhere—blue and yellow and pink.

Helen tipped back her head. She spread her arms wide and fell back. Her bare arms lay outspread across the wildflowers. She could smell their sweet fragrance. She closed her eyes. And when she finally opened them, she was looking up into Jim's blue eyes.

Eyes as blue as the sky behind his head. Into her upturned hand he placed something cool. Without looking, she closed her fingers around it. She brought it to her mouth. Her teeth bit into the slice of orange.

Before she had opened her eyes she had smelled the orange. She had known that it was being peeled for her. She had smelled the oil in the skin as it was torn from the fruit. So she'd been ready when Jim placed the slice into her palm.

He fed her like that—one piece at a time. He waited until she had chewed the very last slice, and swallowed. Then he bent down. He smelled the orange on her breath as he kissed her.

They spent a long hour on that grassy bank of wildflowers and moss. Then they started back across the lake.

The slow glide of the canoe gave the feeling of a dream. Helen's black hair spilled over Jim's lap, over his knees. She sat on the bottom of the canoe, nested between his legs as he paddled. When she finally spoke, it was in a voice as gentle as a whisper. "Tell me, what was her name—your wife?"

She knew that she was asking for a secret. She waited.

"Her name was Ruth."

Helen repeated the name with the greatest of care. "Ruth."

Jim dipped the paddle in on the left side. Then he crossed over to the right. The drips fell across Helen's bare legs.

"Am I getting you wet?"

"I like it."

He let the canoe glide for another long moment. His free hand stroked the long black hair that spilled across his knees. "I like your name. 'Helen.' It sounds so strong. Wasn't there a famous woman in history named Helen?"

"Yes. Helen of Troy. A war was fought because of her. Thousands of men were killed." It was now her turn to tease, and she tipped back her head and looked up into Jim's face, upside-down. "But that couldn't happen now, in these days."

"Helen?"

"Yes?"

"Do you feel guilty?"

"For making love with you? No. I'm too happy to feel guilty yet."

Jim Bass dipped the paddle in and the canoe surged forward. He was glad that Helen couldn't really see his face. "Some people believe that it's bad luck to speak of being happy."

"Do you believe that?"

"Maybe. It might be tempting the gods."

"So if I say aloud that I am now happier than I've ever been in my life—a bolt of lightning will flash down out of the sky."

"Something like that."

"Jim, look at the sky."

He looked up. She was right. The sky was a perfect blue. Not a single cloud. No black thundercloud to hurl down a bolt. "Helen, do you remember that first letter you wrote me? About your husband wanting to hire a plane?"

"I blush to remember that letter."

"I just thought it so strange."

"Oh Jim, don't spoil things. I know what you're going to say." She put her hands over her ears.

"What seemed strange was that your husband had you write the letter for him. And it didn't seem to bother you. You took it for granted that a wife was like…"

Helen lowered her hands from her ears. "A servant?" Her voice had grown tight.

"That letter touched me. I knew you were caught. And you seemed to have so much life inside you. Your letter bubbled over with life."

"I had spring fever."

"But what about William? You sounded so lonely in that letter."

"You want to know about William? I'll tell you. For so many years I worshipped him. He was going to be a great artist. And I was going to help him. He was going to devote his life to art, and I was going to devote my life to him."

"So it's true. You're caught."

Helen bowed her head. She was silent for a long time. Then she lifted her gaze. "I *was* caught."

Helen shifted in the canoe, turning to face him. She sat with her legs crossed under her. The loose dark hair fell about her shoulders.

"Jim? Remember when I said that I'd never been happier than now, here, with you? Well, there was one other time."

"When was that? Should I brace myself?"

"It was the day that I brought Billy home to live with us. He was thin and small and scared. But I knew that I could make him better." Helen looked up at Jim. It was almost as if she was pleading her case, all over again.

"He never cried. I think he was beaten as an infant. He never said a single word until he was four years old. Then one day he spoke a full sentence—he just came right out with it." Helen smiled at the memory. "I guess he finally felt it was safe to talk."

"Does Billy know that he's adopted?"

"Oh, I've told him. But he's still so young. He doesn't really understand." Helen stared off to one side, frowning. Jim could see that she was thinking of Billy.

He studied her profile. Slowly her gaze softened. Her voice grew even softer as she stared off over the water: "Jim, why does it seem as if I've known you all of my life?"

It wasn't a question. There was no answer. It was a mystery.

Helen spoke to a far point across the water. "You feel that way too, don't you?"

He nodded, yes.

*F*ragile

There is another sticker you can ask for at the post office. It has the word "Fragile" printed on it. Use this sticker whenever there is something special inside a package that you're mailing.

The Fragile sticker is a message for the people who work for Canada Post. It tells them to handle your package with care. Don't drop it. Don't toss it into a bin along with the other packages, don't let it be crushed under their weight.

You might want to put two Fragile stickers on your package. Glue one on the front and one on the back, just to be safe. These stickers are used mostly on packages.

But a Fragile sticker is sometimes glued to a letter, before it gets sent off. The sticker is a message to the person who will open the letter and read it.

In this case, the word "Fragile" is a plea. The plea is, "Handle this letter with care, for my heart is inside. *Don't drop it, don't crush it, don't toss it into a bin.* "

You're worried that your heart might get broken.

6

At 2:30 that afternoon, Helen was in the garden picking strawberries. Any moment now, the school bus would be dropping Billy off at the bottom of the driveway.

Helen squinted up at the sun, judging the time. Then she bent to her work again. A half-full bowl of strawberries rested in the dirt beside her. Her small hands darted under the green leaves of the strawberry plants.

Soon came the hollow banging of Billy's empty lunch box. It was banging against his leg as he walked up the drive.

Helen smiled to herself. She was waiting for the moment when he noticed the floatplane, down at the end of the dock.

The banging stopped. Billy came running.

"Wow!" He flew through the open gate into the garden. "Mom!" He ran down between the rows of strawberry plants. "The Dragonfly is back!"

She tilted her face up to him. "Where's my kiss?"

"But Mom!" Billy pecked her cheek, then looked around, "Where is he, the pilot, Mr. Bass?"

Helen smiled. She tossed another handful of strawberries into the bowl. "He's staying for supper."

"He is? Wow!" And he ran from her without a backward glance.

Helen watched him go. A calm happiness filled her. Less than five hours had passed since Jim Bass had surprised her in the laundry room. And now he was up in her kitchen. Helen found herself thinking of the hour that they'd spent together upon the wildflowers.

Even if she never saw him again, that hour would be enough.

Of course, she was fooling herself. But she had to. She had to pretend that these magic hours today had nothing to do with her other life, her real life.

She walked up to the house, carrying the bowl of strawberries. She'd had just enough time to comb bits of moss from her long black hair and braid it before Billy arrived. But she wasn't aware of the glow of happiness on her face. When she walked into the kitchen, Billy looked up. He studied her for a moment. "Mom, you look different."

"How do I look different?" she asked. But she glanced quickly over at Jim, and their eyes met.

Billy was still peering up at his mother. "Well… you look pink."

Helen laughed. "Do I?"

"Yup." Then he called over his shoulder. "That's too tight, Mr. Bass."

Jim was tying an apron around Billy's waist. "Is that better?"

"Yup." Billy climbed up on a stool at the counter. "I'm helping Mr. Bass. I get to cut the mushrooms."

Helen nodded. "I see that." She still held the bowl of strawberries. And yes, her cheeks felt warm, and were probably pink. Steam filled the kitchen. And the good smell of garlic and onion being heated in butter.

Billy turned on his stool. "Mr. Bass? Why are you cooking supper for us?"

"I'm trying to impress your mother, Billy."

The boy nodded, "Oh."

"Where shall I put these strawberries?" asked Helen. The counter was already crowded with vegetables and pans. She was lost in her own kitchen. It was a wonderful feeling.

"Over here," Jim cleared a spot for the bowl. "You told me to raid the fridge for anything I needed. Billy and I are making spaghetti sauce."

Then he turned and placed his big hands on Helen's shoulders. She let herself be gently pushed towards the table.

"I guess I'm supposed to stay out of the way." She sat down. In front of her stood a bottle of wine. Red wine. The cork lay to one side. "Jim! Where did this come from?"

"I brought it with me in the plane. Just in case I was asked to supper." Jim looked around the kitchen. "But I couldn't find any wine glasses in the cupboard."

"No," said Helen. And she added quietly, "William doesn't like wine." She looked down at her hands in her lap. Then she lifted her head, and smiled. "But I like it."

Red wine was poured into a small juice glass in front of her.

"Thank you." She took a sip. The wine slipped smoothly down her throat. She smiled. "I feel like I'm at a party."

Jim stepped back, pleased. His broad tanned face was stretched in a grin. He hitched up his pants. His sleeves were already rolled up past his elbows. His wavy brown hair was damp at the temples. "There's one more thing that I need while I cook."

"What? What can I get you?" Helen started to rise from her chair.

Jim put his hands on her shoulders. "No. You just sit down." He stepped back again. "What I need is some music. We're cooking Italian food. We need Italian music. But I couldn't find any record player, or tape deck. Nothing. What about a radio?"

"Mr. Bass?" Billy piped up, "I finished cutting."

"Just a minute, Billy, I'll be right there." Jim turned back to Helen. "No radio?"

Helen giggled, shaking her head. "William threw the radio out last month. He decided that it brought too much bad news."

Back at the counter, Jim swept the mushrooms into his hand. "Good job, Billy." He tossed them into the cast-iron pot on the stove. Billy turned on his stool. He looked down into the pot of sauce. "Mr. Bass, I'm not going to eat any of that red stuff. I want just white spaghetti."

Jim shrugged. "Fine. Now watch while I chop the parsley."

The wine had warmed Helen's stomach. Now it was going to her head. She called across the kitchen: "Mr. Bass, where did you learn how to cook?"

"In the Navy, Ma'am."

In the Navy. Helen blushed. She remembered the tattoo she had seen on his bare shoulder, during that hour on the grassy bank.

"Helen, you can pour me a small glass of that wine—but that's it. I have to fly back to Grand Forks tonight. I'll need to keep a clear head." Jim lifted the chopping knife into the air: "Opera! That's what we need!" And in a deep voice he started singing in Italian. Under the table, Potto lifted his head, and his ears, and began to whine.

"Mr. Bass, Mr. Bass!" cried Billy. He grabbed at Jim's arms. "My dad won't like it. You gotta be quiet."

Jim broke off his song.

Billy's face wore a look of concern. "Dad's up in the attic, Mr. Bass. You can't make any noise when he's painting."

"Billy?" Helen called softly.

"What?" The tense look was still on his small face.

"Your father isn't here."

"He's not?"

"No. He drove down to Spokane with his new painting."

The boy's face now showed a mix of emotions. There was relief. And there was a look of longing, as he turned his gaze from his mother to Jim, and back again. "When will Dad—"

Helen rushed in with the words. "He'll be back tomorrow, Billy."

Potto was also concerned. He had stationed himself at the door. He turned his sad eyes in Helen's direction.

"Don't worry, Potto, he'll be back tomorrow." Helen was feeling the wine. She spoke her thoughts aloud. "You love me and you love Billy, don't you Potto. But William is top dog in this house."

A silence followed. Then came the sound of the knife on the chopping board. As Jim chopped, he began to hum a tune.

Dessert was strawberries in a big bowl. Billy eyed the bright red berries in the middle of the table. Helen went first. She picked out a strawberry from the bowl. Then she dipped it into the bowl of whipped cream. She closed her eyes as she put the berry on her tongue.

"Good?" asked Jim. He grinned as he watched Helen. She kept her eyes closed for a moment as she tasted the sweetness.

"Ah, yes," Jim wagged his head, "I love to eat." He dipped a big red strawberry into the cream and popped it into his mouth.

He and Helen now eyed each other. She'd told him about Billy's refusal to eat anything but white foods. He liked mashed potatoes, milk, the white meat of chicken, Cheerios. He would eat bananas and apples, but only if they were peeled first.

"Mmm," Jim murmured, and reached for another strawberry.

Billy watched the bush pilot's big hand. Then his own small hand darted into the bowl. His fingers found a tiny berry. He didn't bother with the cream. The strawberry went straight into his mouth. He bit down once, twice. His eyes were big. Then he spit it out onto his hand. "Look!" He held out the chewed strawberry. "I did it!" And he gazed with pride at the tiny red mound on his palm.

Jim laughed. "Well done, Billy."

Billy's smile spread from ear to ear on his freckled face. His reddish hair was hanging down over his eyes. His eyes were shining.

Jim and Helen exchanged a glance.

"Sweetheart, I'm proud of you. How did it taste?" Helen reached across to smooth Billy's hair back from his brow.

The boy squinted, "Not very good."

It was Helen's turn to laugh. "Oh Billy," and she leaned across and kissed his forehead. "It's time that I gave you a haircut."

A kitchen chair was carried out to the front lawn. They found a level spot on the slope. Billy sat down. A sheet was drawn around him and tied at the back of his neck.

"Ready?" asked Helen.

But Billy wasn't listening. "Mr. Bass, how old were you when you learned to fly?" The pilot sat cross-legged on the lawn in front of him.

"Well, how old are you, Billy?"

"Seven," the boy answered, with a blush at his freckled cheeks.

"Let me see… I was 12 years older than you when I flew my first plane."

"You mean I have to wait *12 years*?"

"Billy, hold still." Helen was parting his hair with a comb. Then she started cutting with her scissors. "Close your eyes."

The boy sat for his haircut with his eyes squeezed shut. Clippings of reddish hair fell to the sheet that covered his lap. The sun was at a low angle in the sky. Its last beams shone on the hair clippings that fell from the scissors. The bits of hair gleamed red-gold as they drifted down.

"It will soon be the longest day of the year," said Jim, as he watched. He was speaking to Helen, though he kept his gaze fixed on the scissors in her hand.

The scissors stopped for a moment. Helen squinted at the setting sun. "Yes, in about three weeks. And where will you be?" She tried to keep the question light.

"Where will I be on Midsummer Eve?" Jim waited until the scissors started cutting again. "I'll be in the Yukon."

"Where's the Yukon, Mr. Bass? Is it far away?"

"Don't move, Billy. Please." Helen found that her fingers were trembling as she held the scissors.

"It's not too far, Billy. But don't worry, I'll be back." Jim was also answering the question in Helen's eyes. "I'll be back," he repeated. "I promise."

"Why are you going to the Yukon, Mr. Bass? Why can't you stay here?"

"Because I have a job, Billy. A man has hired me. He's a miner, and I have to fly him into the bush to work his claims."

"What are claims?"

Helen bit her lip. "Billy, you're done, sweetheart." She untied the sheet from around his neck. "Now go brush your teeth. And get your pajamas on."

"But Mom!" the boy protested. Then he turned to the bush pilot. "Will you still be here when I get back?"

Jim nodded. He watched the boy run up the slope.

Helen was holding the sheet to one side of the empty chair. "Next?" she said brightly. But even she could hear the tremble in her voice.

Jim didn't move from where he sat on the lawn. "Are you offering me a haircut?"

She nodded, "Yes." She tried to smile. She joked, "They say that when a woman cuts a man's hair, the man is then under her spell."

"I already am," he said quietly. His broad, tanned face was serious.

Helen couldn't trust herself to speak.

Jim then spoke in a voice hoarse with emotion. "Do you cut William's hair?"

Helen bowed her head. "Yes." She knew what Jim was asking. "But not for months."

Jim stood up from the lawn. He came forward and sat down, facing away from Helen. His bulk filled the wooden chair. He seemed so large, compared to Billy's small form. Helen held the sheet in her hands. She felt suddenly shy.

Jim sat with his hands on his knees, waiting.

She bent to wrap the sheet around him. He grabbed her arm. "Helen…"

The kiss was long. And even a bit awkward, with Helen leaning in from the side. Jim let go of her arm. Still she kissed him. Then she straightened with a gasp. "Oh my."

She looked around: "Where are my scissors?"

Helen picked up the scissors from the lawn. Her heart thumped in her chest. She took a deep breath. Then, with the scissors in her hand, she studied Jim's thick wavy hair. Finally she forced herself to make the first cut.

A lock of brown wavy hair fell to Jim's shoulder.

Oh dear, thought Helen. She dared another cut with the scissors. Then she laughed at herself. "Maybe it's the other way around, Jim."

"What do you mean?" He sat with the sheet tied around his neck.

"It might be the woman who falls under the man's spell, when she cuts his hair."

"That sounds good to me," he replied.

"Hold still!" she said with mock sternness.

"Yes, ma'am."

As each lock of hair fell from her scissors, Helen could have wept. She didn't cut too much. When the haircut was over, she gathered the clippings together in the sheet.

"Where are you going with my hair?" Jim called. He watched as she shook the sheet open next to a rose bush. The hair clippings fell to the soil.

"It helps to keep the deer away," said Helen. "They smell the human presence." Then she folded the sheet, folding it into a small square.

"How do I look?" Jim called. He still sat in the chair, his hands on his knees.

A man with a fresh haircut can have a shorn look. His ears might seem a little bigger, and appear to stick out more. Helen smiled. She had only given him a trim, but she'd been right: it's the woman who falls under the spell of the man. Because after she cuts his hair, she sees the boy in him, and her heart melts. "You look… younger."

She held the folded sheet against her chest. Then she asked the question that had been hovering in her mind. "When do you leave for the Yukon?"

Jim stood to his feet and hitched up his pants. "Tomorrow."

The news hit her in the stomach. "Tomorrow!"

"Oh, I almost forgot." Jim reached into the pocket of his shirt. "Here's the receipt you asked for."

He saw the blank look on her face. He stepped closer, and he added softly, "It's the receipt for your husband's plane ride."

She took the piece of paper. She thrust it into the pocket of her white shorts.

"Helen, I—"

But Helen's attention was elsewhere. "Billy," she called, "why are you bringing those blankets out?"

"…love you," said Jim.

The fragment of speech hung in the air between them.

"Mom, can I sleep outside on the dock tonight, next to the Dragonfly?"

Helen was now staring up into Jim's blue eyes. "Yes," she said.

"Hoo-ray! Mom, will you sleep outside too, like last summer?"

"Yes," she answered, still looking up at Jim.

The sun had been down for an hour by the time Jim could force himself to leave.

In the twilight, water lapped at the posts under the dock. Billy had brought out the bedding. He lay snug under his blankets. From where he lay, he had a good view of the Dragonfly. And he had a good view of his mother and the pilot. They stood talking quietly on the dock, just out of earshot.

They had been talking for some time.

Helen repeated Jim's question in a low voice, so that Billy wouldn't hear. "Why do I stay?" Helen now turned to gaze out across the lake. Once again she repeated Jim's question in a low voice. "Why do I stay? Oh Jim…" She turned back to him, changing the subject. "It's getting dark."

Jim swallowed. "Yes, I guess I should go. But Helen, think about what I said." He lowered his voice, "People divorce. They remarry."

A flash and a bang lit up the sky—the explosion made them both jump. They grabbed at each other for balance.

Jim's voice was shaky. "Jeez. What was that?"

"Mom!" yelled Billy, sitting up in his blankets.

But Helen began to laugh. Her light laugh floated out over the lake. She couldn't stop. She clutched the front of Jim's shirt. She laid her head against his chest, still laughing.

Finally she choked out, "It's our mailbox!" And gasping, added, "It's jinxed!"

Helen and Billy slept on the dock that night in their sleeping bags. Potto slept nested between them. It was a little past dawn when a sharp voice cut through Helen's dream.

"Helen! What are you doing out here? Can't you see that it's going to rain?"

It was William's voice, and it was angry.

Helen sat up in her sleeping bag. Her dark hair fell wild around her shoulders. She blinked. "William, what's wrong?"

"You know damn well what's wrong, Helen."

Billy sat up and rubbed his eyes. "Dad? Is the Dragonfly gone?"

William was now pacing along the edge of the dock. He shook his fist in the air. "That new mailbox cost over $70, plus the wages we paid to that good-for-nothing kid." William paused. "Helen, are you listening? Do you hear what I'm saying? Our new mailbox is gone."

She nodded, dazed.

"What time did it happen?"

"What time?"

"You *must* have heard the blast, Helen! There's not a scrap left of that mailbox! It's been blown to a thousand pieces!"

Helen was awake now. A wind stirred the birch trees along the shore. A distant rumble of thunder sounded. She closed her eyes and felt the fresh wind on her face. She still dwelled in her dream—of Jim. Nothing that William might say could take away her happiness. She drew a deep breath. The wind smelled so good.

She opened her eyes. William was standing above her. He was trembling all over. Helen could see that it wasn't just from anger. "William! You're frightened. What is it?"

"I'm not frightened." He ran his hand back through his white hair. Then he turned to her again. "Do you think that this is

Monty's doing? He must be out of the hospital by now. It could have been him." He paused to think. "Where were you when you heard the blast?"

Where had she been? Helen's thoughts returned to the night before. Into her mind came the image of Jim's face, as he talked quietly to her on the dock.

"Helen?"

She blushed. "I... I think it was around nine o'clock last night that we... that I heard the blast."

"Dad! Mr. Bass was here! And I helped him cook supper. And look—" Billy searched under his pillow. "He gave me this!" The boy held up a small pocketknife. "To keep!"

"Really," said William. He frowned at the sight of the pocketknife.

Helen drew his attention away from the gift. "You're back early, William." She was still sitting up in her sleeping bag. "Does that mean you have good news?"

"The reason I'm back early is because the motel in Spokane was too noisy. I couldn't sleep. I finally got up in the middle of the night and drove home."

Helen pushed the sleeping bag off her lap. "But what about your painting? Do you have a buyer for it?"

"Yes, but they'll have to wait. I've brought the painting back." His face showed a sheepish look as he added, "The painting's not finished, after all."

"Not finished?" Helen was looking up at him in disbelief. "Not finished?" she repeated. Then she bowed her head and buried her face in her hands.

William stood looking down at her bowed head. She was in her nightgown. Her long black hair hung loose and the wind blew it around her shoulders. William tried to keep a level voice. "What did that pilot want?"

Helen spoke into her hands, "He brought your receipt."

"He *brought* my receipt? Couldn't he have just mailed it?"

Helen lifted her face from her hands. "Billy, I want you to go up to the house. Take your blankets. It's going to rain. Potto, you go with him."

The dog wagged his tail, but didn't budge. He was waiting for William's greeting.

But William's attention was on Helen. He glared down at her. "So I suppose he took you up in his plane again."

"We didn't go up in the plane."

"What about your duty to the guests, Helen, and to me?"

"I said we didn't go up in the plane." Helen stood up from the sleeping bag. The wind whipped her long nightgown around her legs.

William towered over her. She looked up at him, meeting his angry stare.

Then he started in pacing again, and waving his arms. "I guess this means that our Mr. Bass will be back. I'll wake up one morning and you'll be off on another joy ride—gone, poof!

"I would never leave Billy." Helen spoke the words with great care.

But William didn't grasp her true meaning. In fact, he wasn't listening to Helen at all. "You'll go off on your joy ride and I'll be left here alone to cope with everything. Who will take care of the boy? And see to the guests? You know I can't spare any time—not a minute. I have to finish this painting. I know I can make it perfect—I *know* I can!" William continued to pace back and forth, lost now in his own thoughts.

"William, it's a good painting." The wind whipped Helen's hair across her mouth, and she pulled it away. "But it's done, it's finished. You'll never capture what you want, you'll never really capture water."

For the moment, Helen had William's full attention. "It can't be done. You can only fail," she continued. "Water is alive. It moves, it flows. It has a… a living essence." Again she brushed her hair away. "A painting is only some colours on a canvas hanging in a room."

But William was no longer listening. Again he paced the dock. Waves now splashed against the posts below. William raised his voice against the wind. "You don't believe in me. You don't believe that I can do it. You've decided that I'm a failure."

"I didn't say that, William. I only said—"

"I heard what you said. You're trying to undermine me, just like Monty Reed. But you know that someone has to look after the house and look after my needs. And you agreed to it." William waved his arms as he paced. "If I'm going to paint, I can't be cooking meals. I can't be…" He searched for an example, "I can't be… ironing pillowcases."

He turned and began walking past her again. "I can't play nursemaid to the guests. Who's going to do the work around here? Who's going to take care of things while I paint?"

"Well," said Helen, with her chin held high, "you could hire someone."

William turned on his heel and slapped her.

For a moment they glared at one another, standing on the dock. That's when the hailstorm hit.

A sudden shower of hailstones fell around them in a noisy clatter. They fell from the sky with such force that Potto began to howl in pain. On his old legs he tried to get away. He struggled up the slope towards the house.

Helen ran from the dock with her arms over her head. The noise was deafening. The white stones pelted her bare arms, stinging her skin.

"Helen! Wait!" William shouted after her.

She ran past the garden. Already the plants were being torn and shredded from the force of the hail. It was as if the sky was falling. The sky had broken and was falling to earth in a million pieces.

The green lawn was now covered in white hailstones. Helen ran over them in her bare feet. She ran for the porch. The metal roof was being pounded with hailstones in a deafening clatter. At the top of the stairs, under cover, Helen paused. She stood shaking in her nightgown. Reaching up with her fingers, she touched her cheek. And she let herself feel it: the sting of William's hand.

*S*pecial Delivery

If your letter carries an urgent message, you can pay extra for Special Delivery. And of course there's a sticker that goes on the letter. A red sticker. Red usually means "STOP." But in the case of a red Special Delivery sticker, red means "GO." Go fast, as fast as you can! Speed to your destination! Take wing!

You've now paid the extra charge for Special Delivery, and the clerk hands you your change. But you don't leave. You stand to one side at the counter. You want to make sure that your letter gets special treatment.

The clerk has your letter in her hand. She takes it over to the sorting table, and pulls open the neck of the canvas sack marked "Special Delivery."

But someone else now arrives at the counter. The clerk thrusts your letter into the canvas sack before she goes to help this new customer.

Your letter is now inside the Special Delivery sack. But the sack gapes open. What if your letter spills out, and ends up on the floor? You wait until the clerk comes back. You watch her close the sack. You want to make sure that she cinches it tight. But she's not moving very fast. In fact, she is moving rather slowly. Far too slowly!

A faster way to send your letter is through a fax machine. It only takes seconds to travel and arrive. Your urgent message will then roll forth on a piece of paper reading, "I'm sorry." Such sorry words. No matter how fast they travel, they always arrive too late.

7

Dearest Jim,

This morning we had a hailstorm. It was terrible and wonderful at the same time. The hail came down so hard that it ruined my roses. The lettuce and spinach have holes all through the leaves. When I went out afterwards to inspect my garden, I almost cried.

I'm lying. I did cry. Some of the tears were because I miss you. I was standing there by the roses and I looked down and saw a lock of your hair on the dirt. I guess it doesn't matter now if the deer come or not.

I keep seeing your face, from when we said good-bye. Remember how I laughed after we heard the explosion? I don't think I've ever laughed that hard. If you're wondering how the mailbox turned out, I'll tell you. The person who did it wasn't William's enemy, the way he thought. It was someone else.

Then the RCMP showed up. They had a teenager with them named Rex. He's a nice kid. I don't think he meant any harm. He was just mad at William for some reason. So Rex and a friend got drunk and blew up the mailbox with a homemade bomb.

Oh, and it turns out that Rex is the person who ran into our mailbox in the first place! That was months ago. I don't think I told you about that. He was driving his parents' green Camaro, and he was trying to turn around in our driveway. Maybe he was drinking that night, I don't know.

The poor kid. He looked terrible this morning when the Mounties brought him to confess. I'm sure he had a hangover. William was pretty hard on him, but he's not going to press charges. Instead Rex has to replace the mailbox.

William got a piece of paper from the Mountie and showed Rex exactly how he wants the mailbox to look. Rex has to make it himself, in Machine Shop at school. While William drew it all out on the hood of the patrol car, Rex kept cracking jokes, even with his hangover. The boy just wouldn't give in. He made me smile in spite of myself.

It was about the only time I've smiled lately. Things are not good between William and me. When a person strikes out at someone close to them, it's not always for the obvious reason. Sometimes it's for another reason that's deeper. I think William knows about us, Jim. In his heart, he knows.

You asked me why I've stayed with him. I want you to know that I don't stay because of money. I'm not dependent on William. I have some income every month from a trust that my father set up. It's not much, but it helps pay for food and clothes and household bills.

You won't read this letter until you come back from the Yukon. There's no way I can talk to you. You're already in the air. The Dragonfly is droning north at this very moment. Jim, please take care. I hope you're thinking of me right now... maybe you are.

Helen folded the letter closed. She stood up from the kitchen table. She was already in her nightgown. Her hair hung long and loose, free of its braid.

Barefoot, she walked to the bedroom and stopped at the open doorway. She didn't go in.

William was sitting up in bed, reading. It was a warm night. He wore no undershirt. On his bare and narrow chest was a patch of white hair.

In the doorway, Helen's arms hung loose at her sides. The fingers of one hand gripped the letter she had just written to Jim. She didn't try to hide it.

"William?"

"Yes?" He took off his reading glasses. "Have you changed your mind?" He tried not to sound too hopeful. "I thought you were going to sleep out on the porch with Billy."

Since the hailstorm, William had been very polite to Helen. They hadn't talked about the slap, but William still wore a sheepish look. In 10 years of marriage he had never struck Helen. And now he had. It was such a terrible fact. The shock was still with them both.

"No, William. I haven't changed my mind. There's something that I have to tell you."

"Oh, no need. No need for an apology, Helen. We all say sharp words once in a while."

Helen knew that this was William's way of saying he was sorry.

He reached over and turned the blankets back on her side of the bed. "Come to bed." He smiled at her—a thin, hopeful smile.

"William, I spent yesterday afternoon with Jim Bass."

"So you said. He left off my receipt. And that's that. We'll say no more about it."

Helen swallowed. She looked down, and fingered the letter in her hand. Then she raised her head. The words now came more slowly. "William, we went for a canoe ride… a long canoe ride," she added, looking straight at him.

"Oh?" William's voice was guarded, and Helen knew that he didn't want her to continue. He didn't want to hear. He didn't want to know what he already knew. He drew back into the pillows, as if trying to avoid what was coming. His eyes grew wide, and his mouth tightened. "Are you saying…"

"Yes." Helen's voice trembled. "I'm saying that we made love."

For a moment, William was speechless. When he found his voice, it was low and filled with venom. "Get… *out*."

Helen remained in the doorway, her heart pounding. She could hardly breathe.

"Get… *out*," William repeated. " *Leave…this…room*."

Helen turned, and was gone, her long hair streaming down her back.

Six weeks had passed since Helen had told William of her betrayal. Six weeks, yet the pain still stabbed fresh whenever William thought of his wife with Jim Bass.

William's only escape was when he was painting. At work up in the attic, his mind could find relief from torturing itself. But it was taking a long time to make his painting of the waterfall perfect. And sometimes the pain would creep back into his mind before he realized why it was there. Then he would remember: Jim Bass.

Today was one of those times, and William's hand began to tremble. He laid down his brush. Slowly he wiped his hands, trying to ignore the hollow pain in his chest. It hurt.

By the time he was walking down the stairs from the attic, anger had come to his rescue.

"Helen!" he called. His voice sounded harsh even to himself. No one was in the kitchen. Out on the porch, two guests sat reading. The screen door slammed behind William.

It was Helen who had been making all the noise. The noise had been buzzing around William's head for the last hour while he'd tried to paint.

The guests looked up from their books. William gave a quick nod, but said nothing.

Down on the sloping lawn, Helen pushed the electric lawn mower across the grass. She wore shorts and a bathing suit top. Her braid was pinned up from the back of her neck for coolness.

She didn't hear William call. She didn't see him as he walked up behind her. Then she turned. William was right in her path. The lawn mower's long orange cord snaked out behind her.

The mower's high whine filled the air. It seemed to William that it was buzzing inside his own head, the buzz of a huge insect. He shouted over the noise. "I want to talk to you!"

"What?" Helen squinted up at him. Her forehead was damp.

William made a cutting motion with his hand. "Turn that thing off!"

The noise faded and died.

William's voice cut through the sudden silence. "Where exactly did you do it, Helen? And where was Billy?"

Helen glanced up at the porch and the two guests who were watching. "William, let's not talk out here."

"Where?! Tell me where you did it. And where was Billy at the time? Did he know what his mother was doing?"

"I told you. He was at school. William, stop." Helen turned towards the lake.

The pain was creeping into William's heart again. And that was something he couldn't bear. He clenched his fists at his sides, clenching his anger. "Is your pilot a better lover than I am? Is that it? How can you prefer someone like him over me? He's a gorilla. He doesn't have a thought in his head." William took a step towards her. "Tell me, what did he do to you that was better than—"

"William stop!" Helen whirled to face him. "It's been weeks now, and you still ask me the same questions." She looked up at the porch. The two chairs were empty. The guests had gone in. Helen glared at her husband. Then her face softened. "Oh, William. Where is your pride?"

What William didn't know was that a cake had been baked for him. At that very moment the cake was cooling in a kitchen cupboard, out of sight.

At supper time that evening, William came down from the attic. He hadn't been able to paint. He had stayed up in the attic all that afternoon because he couldn't face Helen.

"Hi Dad!" Billy sat at the table, his face shining. "He's here, Mom—Dad's here." The boy grinned, then put his hand over his mouth, giggling.

William kept his head down as Helen filled his plate. "Thank you," he muttered.

Helen sat down. "It's a beautiful evening."

William nodded.

The clink of forks could be heard as they ate. It was just the three of them. The two guests had gone off to a cafe in town.

"Don't gobble your food, Billy." Helen gave him a look, and a little smile, "Calm down, honey."

At the end of the meal, William folded his napkin. He pushed back his chair, ready to leave the table.

Billy jumped up. "Dad, you gotta go into the living room. And then you come out when we call you."

William hardly heard him.

"No Dad, not that way."

But William headed out to the porch. The evening air smelled of newly-cut grass. It was a sore reminder to William of the fight with Helen earlier that day. The beauty was still all there: the green lawn sloped down towards the lake and the dock. It was all there, in front of his eyes, but he couldn't feel it. The peace of the evening seemed to mock him.

"Dad, you can come in now!" The screen door swung open. "Dad!"

"What is it, Billy?"

"You have to come in."

The cake blazed with candles. The yellow flames lit up Billy's face and Helen's. Their two voices joined as they sang to William.

He reddened. He'd forgotten his own birthday. The song ended.

Then Billy clutched at his arm. "Dad, I counted out 51 candles, like Mom said. Now you have to blow them all out with one breath."

Fifty-one candles. Was Helen making fun of him, of his age?

"Make a wish, Dad!"

But William made no wish as he blew the candles out, every one. Black smoke rose from the wicks of the candles. The sharp smell filled the kitchen.

Billy began picking the candles from the cake and sucking the white frosting from their tips. Helen cut the cake, and dished out ice cream.

"This is very kind," said William.

Later that night, when Helen came in from putting Billy to bed on the porch, William blocked her way. He'd been waiting behind the screen door.

"I was listening to the story you were telling Billy."

William followed her down the hall. "Is that story connected to your pilot, Helen?"

"It was the story that Billy asked for, William." She went into the bedroom. She reached for her nightgown that hung on a hook behind the door. But William stepped in front of her and closed the door, leaning back against it. His pale face was flushed pink.

"Helen, you always said that you would stand by me."

"And I have," said Helen.

"You won't even sleep in the same bed with me!"

Helen looked down at the floor. "I'm sorry. I just… can't."

"What do you mean, you can't? You *won't*. You're trying to punish me for what you see as neglect."

"William, I'm not trying to punish you. I just can't help how I feel."

"And what is it that you feel? I suppose you think you're in love with that gorilla. Do you really suppose he's going to get involved with a woman who has a son like Billy? That man won't—"

"There's nothing wrong with Billy."

"How can you say that! A boy who will only eat food if it's white. You don't think there's something wrong with that?"

Helen couldn't bear to witness what William was doing to himself. "Billy is so much better, William. Can't you see that?"

"White cake, white candles, white ice cream—"

She cut him off. "The party was Billy's surprise for you."

"You have to face facts, Helen. The boy was strange when we got him, and—"

"William, shut up."

Tears welled up in William's eyes. "—and he's still strange."

"I said, shut up." Helen's voice was fierce. "You're talking about your son."

William looked at her. Slowly his face became pinched. His eyes squeezed shut, and the tears now spilled over. He bent his head towards Helen. A sob shook him as he rested his bent head against her chest.

Helen felt her anger drain away. She put her arms around his thin shoulders. "William, I know that what I did with Jim Bass has hurt you. I'm sorry. I can't change what happened. I can't go back to how things were."

"Yes you can!" William had lifted his head. "Don't sleep out on the porch tonight. Stay here with me."

Slowly Helen withdrew her arms. "William, I can't."

His red and tear-stained face loomed over her. He grabbed her shoulders. "Don't say that."

He was shaking her. Helen clutched her stomach.

Then he let her go. "Oh god, I'm sorry Helen."

She took a deep breath. "I'm sorry too."

William shook his head in wonder at himself, at his own sudden anger. "This can never happen again."

"No. It can't." After a moment, she reached again for her nightgown on the hook. Her hand was trembling as she gripped the doorknob. "Good night."

Helen lay awake for a long time. Her narrow bed was next to Billy's on the porch.

When she turned on her side she could look out and see the stars.

But most of the long hours she lay on her back, thinking, her eyes wide open. She thought of how she had clutched her stomach, when being shaken by William. She'd covered her stomach without thinking, trying to protect it from harm.

Now as she lay on her back, Helen again put her hands on her belly. Her body had known the truth. Now she let the truth come into her mind.

But it's impossible!

She turned on her side again, and looked out at the stars. Jim was always in her thoughts. All day, every day, she thought of him, and her heart ached with longing. After he'd left, she had counted the days until his return. Three weeks, he had told her. Three weeks had passed, and she'd expected any moment to hear a white plane roar overhead.

A fourth week had passed with no letter from him. Then five weeks, six. Not a single word came from Jim. All that time, Helen had hidden her weeping from William. She wept in the bathroom, or in bed, after Billy was asleep—as now. The tears ran across the bridge of her nose and onto the sheet.

Helen turned on her back again, and rested her hands on her stomach. *Can it be possible?*

She recalled a conversation with Jim. They'd been cleaning up the dishes together after their supper. Jim had been washing and Helen was drying. "Are you sure that you can't get pregnant?" he'd asked. Then he'd held up one hand in protest: "I know that you already told me it's impossible. I know that's why you had to adopt." Soap had been dripping from his hand, so he'd put it back into the dishwater.

What Jim said next had made Helen's heart beat fast. And even now, a quiet joy filled her, to remember.

He'd been rinsing a plate, holding it under the running water. He spoke in a whisper. "It's just that today, when we were… lying together, I had the strangest sense that we'd created—"

But before he could say it, Helen had placed her hand over his mouth, saying, "Shhh. I know."

For she had sensed it also.

In the morning, after a restless sleep on the porch, Helen said good-bye to her garden. In the last six weeks it had recovered from the hailstorm. Fresh leaves had replaced those that had been shredded and torn.

The roses were doing well. New buds had formed and opened into sweet-smelling petals. Standing in front of a rose bush, Helen glanced down, and for a moment her heart stopped. A lock of Jim's hair could still be seen lying on top of the dirt. She picked it up—a small tuft of brown wavy hair. She would keep it, for luck.

She did her chores, as on any morning. The last guests left after a big breakfast. William was already up in the attic, so they couldn't shake his hand in farewell. But they shook Helen's hand, and thanked her. "We'll be back next summer."

Helen watched them go. Next summer… She didn't tell them that she wouldn't be here.

"Hello Potto. Is it time for the mail?"

The old dog was already limping down the porch stairs. "Wait for me," called Helen.

It was a perfect summer morning. The sun was already high. A sweet fragrance drifted from the poplar trees. Wild daisies bloomed on the bank along the driveway.

The road was dusty under Potto's paws. He left a trail of prints in the dust, next to prints of Helen's bare feet. She was wearing her favorite dress, the one with tiny green stripes, and her long braid hung down her back. She walked slowly, so that Potto could keep up. They arrived together at the mailbox.

It was a homemade mailbox, welded together with little skill. Its dull grey paint was already starting to peel. Rusted metal showed through. The mailbox had a misshapen red metal flag lying flat against one side. There was no door on the mailbox, no flap. But on one end, a round hole had been cut in the metal, about five inches across. The rim of the hole was jagged and sharp.

This was the mailbox that Rex had built in Machine Shop at school. Helen found herself staring at it. She had been so blind to everything these last weeks that she hadn't really looked at the mailbox.

Rex's mailbox. It was ugly. It was a mockery of William's carefully-drawn plan.

Helen started to giggle. Her laughter floated out on the summer morning. Again, Rex had made her laugh. And even to Helen's own ears it was a happy sound.

She reached her small hand through the hole and pulled out an art catalog. Then a letter from her brother in Vancouver, and a few bills. No letter from Jim, but she hadn't expected one.

"Come on, Potto. Let's go back. I have to start packing."

The dust of the driveway was warm between her toes as she walked. Her heart was light. All the guilt and shame and sorrow of the last weeks was gone. Her step was light also—as light as a dancer's. She had to pause several times for Potto to catch up. Here he came, limping up the road.

"I'm sorry, Potto. Am I walking too fast?" When Potto reached her, Helen squatted down. She took his head between her hands and looked into his bleary eyes. "I shall miss you, Potto. Will you miss us, too?" The dog's tail wagged. His pink tongue panted from his mouth. Helen smiled. "Oh Potto, you have dog's breath." And she kissed him lightly on his black nose.

William laid the bundle of catalogs and envelopes on the kitchen counter. It was a week's worth of mail. This was the first time he had walked out to the mailbox since Helen and Billy had left. He hadn't looked through the bundle yet. His hand was bleeding.

"Jane!" he called out. The sight of the blood made him feel faint.

He'd scraped the back of his hand while pulling the mail out through that tiny hole. *Damn* Rex!

The new housekeeper hurried into the kitchen. "What is it, Mr. Turner?"

"Bring me a Band-Aid... please," he added, when she didn't move. Jane had been hired to look after the bed-and-breakfast. The girl was home from college for the summer. She could only work until September. Then she would be going back to school. What would happen to him then? He'd have to find someone else, go to all that trouble.

"I've brought you the whole box of Band-Aids, Mr. Turner." Jane set it on the counter.

"Thank you," he called after her. He'd wanted her to bandage the cut for him, but didn't dare ask.

At least the bleeding had stopped, though it was awkward using his left hand to put the Band-Aid onto his right.

Then he took the bundle of mail to the table. Potto followed him. Potto followed William everywhere, these days.

Sunlight flooded in through the window. William pushed the shutter closed. The sunlight now fell in slats across the table, and across the pile of mail. William began to shuffle through the envelopes and flyers. A postcard fell from the folds of a catalog.

The postcard was from Helen.

William's heart raced. But he didn't read it. Instead, he looked through the rest of the mail, as if the postcard held little importance. It was then that he spied the letter. It was addressed to Helen

Turner. And up in the left-hand corner was the sender's name: Jim Bass.

As William sat there, staring, something warm was pressing on his leg. Potto had placed his chin on William's knee.

William reached down absently to pet the dog's ears. He took a deep breath. He decided to read the postcard first.

Dear William,

We're both fine, we're staying at my brother's in Vancouver for now. You can write to Billy at this address. There is a saying that "Time heals all wounds." I hope that is true. I will always respect you. Believe me when I say that I never meant to hurt you.

Helen

William put the postcard back on the table beside the other mail.

Helen's postcard now lay next to the letter from Jim Bass. The letter he'd addressed to Helen. Was it a crime to read other people's mail?

William tore open the envelope. His long fingers trembled as he unfolded the pages of handwriting. He felt like a spy. He was spying on the man who had stolen his wife away. But it was really into Helen's heart that he was spying...

I'm not able to write this letter, the nurse is writing it for me. My brain is still foggy. The nurse says I've been in this hospital bed for two weeks. I'm pretty thin, sweetheart. I think I'm going to need suspenders to hold up my pants when I get out of here. After the plane went down we ran short of food. We lived on berries and grubs and whatever we could find.

And then the handwriting changed:

My darling Helen. As you can see, my hand is pretty shaky. I'm getting better. This is my second day with a clear head. The nurse said she will mail this letter for me. I made her promise to mail it today. Never never never think that I have deserted you. That is what worried me most. We were in the bush for 15 days. We had trouble right from the start. The miner who hired me wasn't always sure of where his mining claims were. He had a lousy map. He kept saying, "Lower, lower."

"Excuse me, Mr. Turner."
William thrust the letter under a catalog. "What is it, Jane?"
"The washing machine is not working."
"Can't you fix it? Is it plugged in?"
The girl rolled her eyes.
"All right, I'll have a look at it later. Is there something else that you can do in the meantime?"
"I can vacuum. But you said it was too noisy."
"Please—go ahead."

And it was under the loud roar and whine of the vacuum cleaner that William bent his head to the letter…

I should have known better than to fly so low. At the wrong moment a downdraft hit us. In the crash, the Dragonfly's tail section broke right off.

My passenger went to pieces. He started praying out loud and confessing all his sins to me. My thought was to get us out of the plane before it caught fire. The guy babbled like a baby. He confessed that he'd once killed another miner in a fight. It was over some claim, I guess. Then he confessed that he'd blown up a miner's truck with the miner in it—that happened over your way.

He kept babbling all this and crying. So I socked him on the jaw and dragged him out. The plane didn't blow, she just lay there, with her broken tail. I've got insurance, but at that moment it didn't help.

Helen, the nurse is waiting to take this page and I haven't said the most important thing. I just want you to know I'm safe and that I'll be coming to get you. I don't care what's right or what's wrong. I've gone over and over this in my mind. Do you remember when you were cutting Billy's hair and I sat on the lawn to watch? I felt like we were a family, the three of us. That's what I want, Helen. I want you and Billy.

William folded the page along its creases. He slid it back into its envelope, the one that he'd ripped open in his haste.

Then he went looking for a larger envelope, and a stamp. The roar of the vacuum cleaner rose and fell as the girl crossed the living room carpet, back and forth. William could hardly hear himself think.

He wet a stamp on his tongue and glued it to a big envelope. On the envelope he copied Helen's new address from the postcard.

Then he walked back down to the mailbox. He carried the envelope in his bandaged hand.

Helen would see that the letter inside from Jim had been opened and read. She would know that it was William who had read it and sent it on to her. And by this she would know that William had let her go.

Reaching the mailbox, William carefully slipped the letter through the jagged hole—pulling his hand out safely. For a moment he glared at the mailbox, and cursed it.

Then he raised the homemade red flag.

*F*lyers

Flyers arrive in the mail all the time. These sheets of paper are often printed in bright colours, to attract your eye. They announce a sale at the hardware store or the supermarket. Or the Mayor might send a flyer asking you to vote for him again. Or a notice arrives to announce that electrical service will be shut off from 10:00 a.m. to 3:00 p.m. on the following Sunday. This is annoying.

The happiest announcement to receive in the mail is one that gives news of a birth. Often there's a drawing of a stork carrying a baby in a sling from its beak.
Sometimes the new parents have a special card printed up. It might be a joke card. If the father works in the post office, the card might joke that the baby was delivered in a mail sack. Or the card might be very fancy, with gold lettering on cream-colored paper.

But sometimes a birth announcement is very simple. The happy parents' names are printed at the top:
Helen and Jim Bass
And then the announcement goes on to say that
On February 28, 1989,
a little sister for Billy arrived,
weighing 6 pounds & 6 ounces.
Her name is Lily,
and she plans to stay.